MW01008496

Shattered Illusions

Shattered Illusions
1st Edition
Copyright 2024 Sammy C

ISBN: 9798883919533

This book is dedicated to my inspiration, Sammy C number 1 & 2. I love you both. As well as all my favorite kids! You know who you are!

The Dome Level One

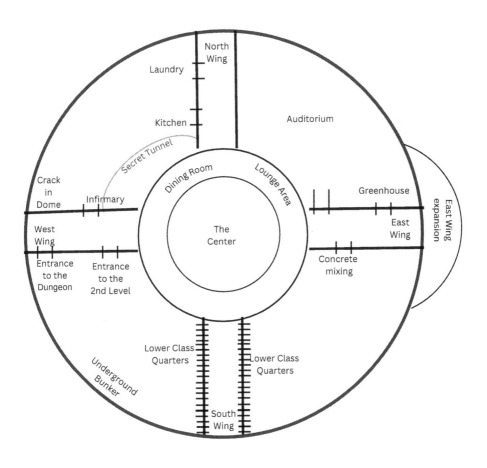

North Wing

Laundry

Kitchen

Auditorium

Secret Tunnel

Dining Room

Lounge Area

Crack in Dome

Infirmary

Greenhouse

East Wing expansion

The Center

West Wing

East Wing

Entrance to the Dungeon

Entrance to the 2nd Level

Concrete mixing

Lower Class Quarters

Lower Class Quarters

Underground Bunker

South Wing

Chapter 1

Abruptly, I was awakened by an excruciating pain resonating throughout my entire body. I couldn't put together any thoughts other than make it stop. My vision was blurred by the intense pain. Still, I tried to will my eyes to focus on the clock across the room. Faintly, I could see the numbers but my mind was too distracted by the pain to be able to put them together in any recognizable order.

I struggled and fought against my body to raise my hands and push them against my ears. I felt as though I was crushing my own skull but the pain would not subside. The noise was so deafening! Somehow, I was able to make out the clock. It read 3:20 AM. What could be going on at this time of the night when everyone is supposed to be sleeping?

There was a protocol for this. We had to assemble in the amphitheater located in the heart of the Dome. I wasn't sure how anyone was going to be able to make that trek with the pain-inducing alarm sounding. In my 11 years of life in the Dome, I have never heard this sound. The Dome is the safest place to be on the entire planet. The only safe place remaining. Greedy corporations made sure of that. Removing every last drop of drinkable water and breathable air from our midst.

One man fought back and protected a small group of us. The Corporation called us rebels. But all we wanted to do was survive. I was only four years old when VI-Count succeeded against the Corporation. He has proven to be our leader and protector. I only know of the outside world now because of what I picked up from the Nobles, and what I can faintly piece together in my mind from life before the Dome.
Nobles are what we call the older ones who live in the Dome. The lower class, that's ones like me, hope to one day reach Noble status. Then, we will be able to gain even more knowledge of the time before and to be able to train others. It's critical to keep order for the survival of the Dome as well as those who reside under its protective walls. VI-Count has made it exceedingly clear that there is no life or protection outside the Dome's walls.

As I continue to try to explore possibilities of what may be causing the alarm, a hand reaches out and roughly grabs me by the shoulder. It's Shawna. She's in the lower class tier like me. But she's 6 and a half, six months older than me. She never lets me forget it! Her parents "disappeared" when VI-Count was trying to break free from the Corporation and its bloodthirsty hands.

We both were only four when we lost our parents amid that escape. I don't remember much about mom and dad. Except that I have my mom's ocean-like blue eyes and her peaceful smile. I also have mom's dark brown hair and dark complexion. I have my father's build, which I am grateful for. There's a lot of work to be done in the Dome. We have to continue to expand to make room as the population continues to grow. Shawna remembers a bit more than me since she is six months older. I catch her staring off at times in the middle of lunch. When I gently pull her back she shares with me sometimes what she was lost in thought about. Shawna tells me about her mom and how she was rather feisty and at times overly confident. She was full of

5

passion which was why VI-Count recruited her for his plans.

She was tall slender built with cool grey purpose-filled eyes. Shawna said she'd love to look into her mom's eyes so full of hope. Shawna tells me it made her feel safer than any old rusty Dome could ever make her feel. Shawna isn't a fan of the Dome. She views it more as a prison. Sometimes I have to agree with her. It does feel like the walls are getting smaller instead of increasing in size. Maybe it's because we are growing up. I don't know for sure. Other times the Dome looks so grand and powerful. I feel like she couldn't be more wrong.

Shawna's father was on the shorter side, brains not brawn as I like to say. Yes, I have muscle but I also have brains. I'm a rare breed, having the best of both worlds. Not to brag. Shawna's father had jade-green eyes which were gentle and welcoming. Shawna tells me that she used to love to snuggle up close to her father who always had the scent of fresh aftershave. Much different from my father who had not so much a scent but an odor of mechanical

grease and sweat, are not something you really want
to snuggle up to.

My head begins to ache even harder, if that's even possible as a bangs against a nearby wall bringing me back to the present. Shawna was still dragging me along down the corridor. It's hard to believe someone so slender as her mother could be so powerful. Even dragging someone like me with my statue down the hall. Shawna is definitely someone you wouldn't want to get on the bad side of. She is much like her mother in that way.

I didn't understand why Shawna wasn't reeling with pain like me and many others until I saw the earplugs in her ears. That explains why she didn't respond to my pleas to slow down. Or the yelp I let out when she hit my head against the wall. I think I feel a little blood trickling down the side of my face! The sight of the blood made me feel a little dizzy. I really hope I don't have a concussion.

When we finally make it to the amphitheater everyone that lives in the Dome is

here. The Nobles were all on their elevated stations
and the lower class well, down in the lower section. Everyone is in such a frenzy. Apparently, I am not the only one who has never heard the alarm. Just as the alarm grows silent VI-Count enters the room.

I am finally able to lower my hands from my ears but my head is still throbbing. My hands seem to be stuck in an odd position from clenching my ears for what seems like an eternity. Shawna gave me an odd look as she carelessly pulled out her earplugs like she was ready for this, acting like the last half an hour was totally normal. Shawna had the ability to make totally off-the-wall situations seem like any old normal day.

We all listened closely as VI-Count began to speak.

"Citizens of the Dome. It gives me great displeasure to inform you all that there has been damage done to the Dome. The west side of the Dome." An audible gas filled the amphitheater from all.

"Impossible!" One Noble called out.

VI-Count continued, "We already have a crew working on it as we speak. Our best welders, Lucas and Aki."

"How did this happen?" A lower class called out.

VI-Count glared, he did not like when the lower class tried to have a voice.

"At this point, we are not sure. But I guarantee we are all safe, "VI-Count reassured the crowd.

"Why the alarm then?" Called out another lower class.

This was all that VI-Count could take, he bit down hard on his lip and responded.

"The alarm automatically goes off if there's any damage ever done to the Dome. We held this assembly to reassure all of you that we are safe and repairs are underway. You may all return safely to your quarters everything is under control."

With that announcement, VI-Count and the Nobles quickly left the amphitheater. The lower class lingered and talked in low, hushed whispers among themselves for a little while before returning to their quarters. Three of the other lower-class kids were deep in conversation. We inched closer to see if we could overhear some of what they were saying. They didn't even notice us as we approached. Tyler and Dimitri were looking as if they were having a bit of a disagreement with Maddy.

"Did you get any commutation from Quinn?" Tyler asked Maddy harshly.

" I haven't heard from Quinn for over a month, it's like he just disappeared!" Maddy said.

"It's not her fault Tyler, don't be so rude!" Dimitri said defensively.

"She's the one who almost got us caught when we were helping Quinn last time. How do we know he's safe, how do we know anything? We can't because of Maddy!" Whispered yelled Tyler.

His face was full of anger and frustration. His green eyes were mere slits as he barked out his furry at Maddy. Although Tyler was sporty Maddy did not back down. This was a new side of Tyler for me and Shawna. Don't get me wrong we really don't know the kid, but what we usually see from him is a kid that is laid back, yet prideful.

"It could have happened to any of us!" Claimed Dimitri.

Shawna and I both looked at each other, curious as to what was going on between these three. Dimitris's deep brown eyes were full of termination not to back down. He was not some pushover. He was a bit nerdy and he loved to tinker, but he was also an apprentice welder and he could hold his own. Maddy was getting ready to respond when I let out a small sneeze. I couldn't help myself I held it in as long as possible. Shawna shut daggers at me through her eyes! We were back behind the petition so they could not see us, I hoped.

All at once they stopped talking and quickly walked away without another word!

"Do you think they saw us?" questioned Shawna.

"I don't think so," I said cautiously.

I was more than happy to return to my own bed after that but Shawna wasn't satisfied. She felt like VI-Count was hiding something. She wanted to explore and find the damaged site. The conversation made Shawna even more convinced something fishy was going on. And who was this Quinn? There was no Quinn in the Dome!

"Shawna we were told to go back to our rooms." I pleaded.

"I know but something isn't adding up! Didn't you see how frazzled VI-Count was? How the young lower-class members lingered for a while. I don't think they trust him. I think they know something else is going on as well. I want to get to the bottom of this, don't you?" Said Shawna

"I would like to get back to bed it's nearly 4:30 in the morning I barely had a wink of sleep!" I said

"But," Shawna went on.

I stopped her. "Fine, but if we get caught I'm blaming you!"

"Whatever," Shawna said exacerbated.

And we were off! We had to go from the auditorium through the Center of the Dome to the North wing. The tunnel was located on the left side near the dining room. We headed along a tunnel that not many even knew existed. It had not been in use for many years. Shawna had stumbled upon it about six months ago. She was sure the tunnel would lead us to the damaged site on the West side of the Dome.

Again I bulked at the idea. I personally don't like small dark creepy enclosed places. But Shawna said it was the only way we would get answers. She told me to stop being a baby and follow her. So I did. We were able to make it almost all the way to the damaged site without anyone seeing us. When we were close we spotted a couple of Nobles standing there discussing the damage. We found it interesting that Lucas and Aki, the welders were nowhere to be found!

No repairs were underway at all. Just a cloud of dust-filled air blowing through the large crack in the glass. We both covered our mouths afraid to breathe in the outside air for we were told that it would be toxic and kill us in a matter of seconds. But here we were still alive minutes later. As well as Nobles who have been assessing the situation for who knows how long.
We touched each other shoulders to make sure it wasn't a figment of our imagination. We slowly took our hands down from our mouths and took in a long slow deep breath after the

Nobles had left. We both coughed a little from the dust but we were alive!

"Why would VI-Count tell us that we could not survive outside the Dome?" Questioned Shawna

"I don't know!" I said sheepishly.

As we were about to leave we noticed a piece of paper down in the corner at the base of the creak. I barely saw it myself, for it was almost completely covered with a fine reddish-brown colored dust that blew in from the outside. I picked it up and dusted it off. Shawna and I looked at each other. Her jade-green eyes were intent and alert. I slowly unfolded the paper and we both gasped. It had our names on it.

Chapter 2

Shawna and I stood in stunned silence for what felt like hours! But in actuality, it was probably only a matter of seconds. I felt as though my heart was going to burst right out of my chest. My ears started to ring from the increase in blood pressure. I started to feel a bit lightheaded, I think I held my breath a little too long! My hands were clenched into tight fists. I was angry, mad, frustrated, and in shock. Confusion overwhelmed my thoughts. mom and dad! But we were told they had "disappeared" thanks to the Corp. How? This has to be a mistake. But there was my name, Sebastian looking right back at me. So many questions were whirling around in my mind.

I glanced over to Shawna to see how she was handling the news. I didn't think she was doing much better than me. I think I might see a bit of blood on the palms of her hands from her fingernails digging into her balled-up fists. Her lips were thin and tight.

Her eyes were mere slits. I think I can hear

her heart pounding even over mine. Which seems impossible! I must be hearing my own pulse reverberating through my ears for there is no way anyone's heart can beat harder or louder than mine. We made eye contact for the first time in what seemed to be hours! Trying to free ourselves from the frozen-like state we can't seem to shake!

"We need to leave here now! It's not safe" Shawna said in a shaky voice.

I couldn't respond audibly, all I could do was nod dumbly. The words they may be watching you replaying in my head over and over again. I can't turn it off. It was haunting my every thought, tangling everything in knots so I couldn't think clearly. I tried but struggled to put one foot in front of the other, but it was taking every ounce of energy that I could muster.
Shawna sees me struggling and grabs me by my shoulder for the second time today and yanks me along. I reflexively raise my hands up to protect my head from any further injury. I had a decent-sized gash from the encounter my head had with the wall not so long ago. Complements of Shawna. Finally, when she felt as though we

were safe she stopped. Looking crushed, she slid her back down the rusty metal wall and crumbled.

Tears were streaming down her face as the shock of the letter and the lack of sleep caught up with her instantly. I had never seen Shawna in a state like that, she was always together, focused. To be honest it scared me! I slid down the cool

metal wall beside her. I put my arm around her trying to comfort her. At the same time wondering who is going to comfort me. We need answers but, how? Shawna was the one to speak up first.

"Sebastian, am I seeing things? Please, tell me you see this too. The words mom and dad?" She was barely audible as she spoke.

"I see it too, It's there! You're not imagining anything!" I soothed to the best of my ability.

The dark unending tunnel seemed to make our feelings even larger. The smell of rust filled our nostrils burning, them along with the stale rank air.

"How could this be?" Shawna nearly whispered.

I did not know what to say. So I remained silent for a bit. As I was trying to sort through the crazy
events of the morning a name popped into my mind. Quinn. Who's Quinn?" I asked perplexed.

"Right! I totally forgot about Quinn!" Shawna said almost excitedly.

Her shoulders were no longer hunched over with confusion. Like I said, Shawna had a way to make weird things seem completely normal. Shawna seemed to be regaining her bearings. It always amazed me how she had this ability! I guess it was a way to help her cope with life, which seemed to be getting more and more confusing by the hour.

"Remember we heard Tyler, Dimitri, and Maddy talking about Quinn!" said Shawna.

"Didn't Maddy say they haven't seen Quinn in over a month?" I asked.

"You're right! We need to talk to them! Right away!" demanded Shawna.

What do I say to that? What is she thinking? We don't even really know them that well. Maddy keeps to herself mostly. She seems to always have a book glued to her nose. I wouldn't say she's shy but more like she doesn't really care about people. Shawna and I seem to be on her most disliked list. Dimitri, well he's off in his own world. He's a serious tinkerer always inventing things for Dome life. A lot of them are really cool, so I hear. But VI-Count doesn't listen to ideas from the lower class no matter how useful it may be. I heard there was a Noble named Louis who had actually stolen a couple of his ideas. Like the water evaporator that has cut back on the Domes water waste by 60%. He is an understudy of Lucas, one of our best welders. Dimitri has never even glanced our way. And Tyler! Well, he thinks he's the coolest person to ever walk in the Dome. He's good at everything he touches. Unlike Maddy and Dimitri who are only 15, Tyler is 16. He is a bit taller than me, but not as muscular by any means. Most people like Tyler. Except for Shawna, who thinks he's conceited and arrogant. These are the three people that Shawna wants us to talk to. How can I talk her out of this? I know with Shawna there's no way to get her to change your mind when she has latched onto an idea.

"How?" That is all that I could muster.

"I don't know. We need a plan!" said Shawna

As we were sitting in the tunnel we began to hear a distant conversation. It was coming from next to the crack in the Dome. We carefully crept down the pitch-black tunnel holding our shaky breath, careful not to let our footsteps reverberate down the rusty tunnel. We only got close enough to be able to barely hear their whispers. Shawna recognized the voices first.

"It's Lucas and Aki!" She mumbled in an undertone

"What a mess! Why would anyone do this?" exclaimed Aki.

"They're sending a message," said Lucas confidently.

"Oh no, do they know about the letter? Is that the message they are talking about?" whispered Shawna, afraid.

I shook my head I didn't think that was what they referring to but I could be wrong.

"What message? What are you talking about?" asked Aki puzzled.

"You have heard the same stories I have. There have been a couple of disgruntled rabble-rousers. They are not happy with VI-Count and they are spreading rumors that life outside the Dome is safe and VI-Count is more power-hungry, greedy, and worse than the Corporation could ever be," said Lucas confidently.

"Who would spread such lies about our protector VI-Count?" Came another voice.

"I was just repeating what I had heard. No harm intended I assure you, Lord Byron," stated Lucas I had never heard the sound of fear in Lucas's voice before. If he being an adult is alarmed how should I feel, how should we feel having a note they could confirm what Lucas was saying? Not only that but also proves that what Lucas was saying wasn't only hearsay. A shock of dread went through my body and I know Shawna was feeling the same thing.

"Lucas, you should beware of what you decide to repeat. It could put you in a dangerous situation. You wouldn't want that, would you? I mean what would Aki do without his fellow welder and friend? Do you understand?" said Lord Byron menacingly.

"Did Lord Byron just threaten Lucas's life?" asked Shawna with indignation in her voice. I can feel Shawna's body engaged ready to come out of hiding and take off Lord Byron's head. I pulled her back before she was fully on her feet. I do have muscles but I cannot do the impossible. I don't know how long I can hold onto her!

"Lord Byron, Lucas didn't realize what he was implying or even what he was saying. I am sure he's just sleep-deprived and shaken up from the early morning alarm. You know that no one has been able to get much sleep lately," said Aki in defense of his co-worker. I was a little taken aback by this. I never really thought Aki liked Lucas. It was a bit odd.

"I will let it slide this time but, if I hear it again I will go straight to VI-Count. Aki will not be able to protect you," Lord Byron said with venom in his voice.

"Yes Sir, I understand," Lucas stated.

Lucas had seemed to lose his voice. When Lord Byron left Lucas and Aki silently went back to work.

"We need to seal the crack, quickly," stated

Aki fearfully.

"You have to watch your tongue Lucas, or you will end up like Toby!" said Aki sadly.

Who is Toby and what happened to him? We know everyone in the Doom or so we thought until today. That's two names in a few hours that we had never heard of. What is going on?

"VI-Count can not get away with this!" said Lucas almost spitting out the words as if they were poison.

"Be quiet you idiot! You know what happens to treasonous people. VI-Count will not allow it! I do not want to be involved in any of this. I do not want to disappear too!" Yelled Aki.

Shawna couldn't take it anymore she jumped out of hiding and went right up to Lucas. There was nothing I could do but go after her.

"What are you so afraid of? What is going on?"

Shawna questioned with fire in her eyes steaming up from her heart.

" What are you doing here Shawna and Sebastian?" Aki asked with intense worry in his voice.

His bald head glistened with sweat. His brown eyes were full of what looked to be terror.

"What did you hear?" Lucas asked a little too forcefully.

A red flush rose over taking his light complexion. I would imagine that Aki had the same heat but it wasn't as evident due to his darker complexion.

"What are you doing?" I whispered out of the corner of my mouth. I could not believe Shawna was doing this!

"Look kids you wouldn't understand!" spat Lucas.

He was not able to contain his irritation at us for listening to the conversation I had with Lord Byron.

"Don't give me that you're just kids you won't understand garbage! Just try me, Lucas!" Shawna demanded.

"Look, I can't really say. Not outright. The closest thing I can get to is this. Things aren't as they seem in the Dome. VI-Count isn't the man he paints himself to be. And Lord Byron, he's just as bad as VI-Count, just as dangerous." Said Lucas cautiously.

"What are you doing Lucas? Is it not enough to put yourself in danger? You're going to go and put these two innocent kids in harm's way right along with you!" Hissed Aki.

Aki was 5'9 but as his anger grew he seemed to be more like 10 feet. I did not like how this was going.

"Look I wanna know the truth. We know some things up. Who is Quinn?" Shawna charged forward.

"How in the history of blue monkeys do you know about Quinn?" asked Lucas in a shocked voice.

"We just overheard that Quinn was with VI-Count," said Shawna coldly.

"With VI-Count?' Lucas repeated with fear and dread in his voice. This was definitely new news to Lucas!

"He must be one of VI-Count's new prisoners". Lucas more thought out loud to himself than to us.

"Prisoners? VI-Count doesn't have prisoners, he. You are not making any sense Lucas," I asked so confused.

Why would VI-Count have prisoners?

Where would he even keep them? We don't have a jail or prison.

"If I say anymore I would be putting you both in danger as my co-worker has so clearly pointed out. I do not want to do that. You have to know that I am probably already being watched," said Lucas coldly.

There it was just like the letter said. He was already being watched. Why? Why was Quinn a prisoner? We needed many more answers to our mounting questions. But we weren't going to get them here. I knew then that Shawna was right. I was not going to tell her that if I could help it. I would never live it down. We would have to talk to Maddy, Tyler, and Dimitri. Lucas made it clear that we needed to leave, so we did.

Shawna and I left without another word returning to the inky black tunnel. A faint familiar smell mixed in with the stagnant air. One that was not there before. It tickled at a memory in the back
of my mind. But I couldn't pull the memory forward. I'd have to let it go for now.
We had bigger problems than a memory
that didn't want to be remembered. I had to jog

to keep up with Shawna who looked like she was a hound hot on a trail. When she was like this there was no way to slow her down. My only chance to keep pace with Shawna was to run.

Chapter 3

I finally caught up with Shawna out of breath from running. Well, running isn't exactly what I would call it. It was so stinking dark in here I couldn't see my hand in front of my face. It was more like I walked at a brisk pace hoping I would not trip on some unseen obstacle. But then again Shawna would find any obstacles before I would. With that thought in mind, I quickened my pace. I know we were nearing the end of the tunnel because Shawna herself slowed. As we were about to step out into the open we heard the loudspeaker crackle to life.

"Attention residents of the Dome. Due to the early morning activity, we are requesting that everyone returns to the quarters. We will resume our assignments tomorrow. We are all in great need of rest. We know that fatigue is one of the leading causes of accidents and here at the Dome safety is vital. We will see everyone during the regular work hours tomorrow. Rest safe."

There was another crackle, then, silence. That was it, the end of the announcement. Never in our lives in the Dome have we ever heard such an announcement? It felt more like we were on lockdown without a choice. Instead of what they were trying to make it out to be. As if it were a vacation day for us to enjoy must needed rest. I was about to say something to Shawna when she reached out and put her hand over my mouth.

I was disgusted and pulled back at once because I knew her hands looked a lot like mine. Covered with who knows what from who knows where. But I knew from the gesture not to say a word. Brains and brawn in action remember. There was Tyler and Maddy but no Dimitri.

"Where is he?" scoffed Tyler.

Tyler seemed to have an all-around bad attitude and generally discussed with everyone. I am not sure why anyone would even choose to be this guy's friend. He talks down to Dimitri and Maddy and every breath. No wonder Shawna doesn't like this guy.

"He'll be here, he told us to stay put!" commanded Maddy.

"We are two out in the open they could be watching us!" reminded Tyler.

"It's less obvious if we are in the crowd. We blend in better than if we were on our own. Then we would stand out like a sore thumb!" Soothed Maddy.

Maybe I was wrong about Maddy. She seems to be able to handle her own. Even the so-called tough guy. She doesn't back down, she just gives it right back to him! A moment later we heard a third voice join them. It was Dimitri.

"Finally, where have you been!" Tyler said angrily.

"It wasn't easy getting to Lucas. He's working with Aki. I had to be careful. I don't trust Aki. He is so overly loyal to VI-Count and seems to worship Lord Byron." Said Dimitri defensively.

"We're glad you were careful and that you're safe." Said Maddy with genuine emotion in her voice.

"Yeah yeah. What did Lucas say?" Tyler asked impatiently.

"Bad news, Quinn has been captured. VI-Count is holding him prisoner." Said Dimitri gravely.

"Oh no, I was afraid of something like that. It's not like Quinn to not deliver his messages," said Maddy with a tremble in her voice.

"How did Lucas know about Quinn? We just talked to him yesterday and he had no idea where he was," questioned Tyler.

"I didn't ask that's not important right now. What's important is that we go to our quarters and stay there like we have been ordered. Lucas said the Watchmen have been told to remain on high alert. VI-Count fears someone has penetrated the Doom. He says everyone will be under tight surveillance. There will be no way to move around undetected," said Dimitri gravely.

"This bites! First, the numbskull VI-Count finds our message delivery system, Aka The Crack. We find out Quinn is being held prisoner and now we are being locked up all day and night!" Snorted Tyler.

"Don't you see? VI-Count is giving himself a perfectly cleared-out Dome. Then he will be able to detect any movement. He must be convinced someone has penetrated the Dome. And that alarm business this morning was planned. The crack was an excuse to get anyone out of his way.

And to cover up what his true intentions are," stated Maddy confidently.

"Brilliant Maddy! That's why Toby wanted you on this mission. I never would've put that piece together! But now I can clearly see it, it makes perfect sense!" declared Dimitri.

"So you're telling me Lucas wants us to sit back and give VI-Count the run of the roost!" Tyler said indignantly.

"Lucas has never led us astray before. We can trust him. We need to do what he says. Besides, if someone from the outside did make it into the Dome we wouldn't want to run the risk of getting them caught. We already lost Toby. And who knows what VI-Count and Lord Byron have planned for Quinn. We have to listen to Lucas. It's for everyone's safety," Maddy said resolutely.

"Did Lucas say anything else?" Tyler demanded.

"No, that was it!" Said Dimitri.

"OK, so it's settled! We go to the cooler until morning!" Said Tyler resigned.

"We are supposed to go to our quarters." Said Dimitri looking confused.

"Cooler is a slang term for prison or penitentiary. People also call at the can or the clink." Maddy spouted off.

"Oh said, Dimitri." With a hint of embarrassment in his voice.

His deep brown eyes look down at the ground to try to conceal his blushing. I kind of got the feeling that this was a regular style of communication with these three. Dimitri is very literal. Tyler trying overly hard to be cool and Maddy with all the book knowledge has an expensive vocabulary able to keep up with the best of them. So far I think Maddy is my favorite. Tyler is way under my skin. I already can't stand him. Well, I'll just leave it at that. Dimitri seems loyal and he's definitely brave. He's all right. Not sure why we ever never really hit it off with any of them before. It's not like the Dome is swimming with options when it comes to friends. It is pretty limited. There are only 5 kids that live in the Dome.

"Tyler, Dimitri, and Maddy! Didn't you three hear the announcement." Louis stated firmly.

"Yes ma'am, we were on our way." Said Tyler boldly.

"Move along then!" Said Louis with a bit too much force behind his voice.

I can feel the hate Dimitri has for Louis from the look he gave him when his back was turned. Making it clear that I definitely did not want to get on Dimitri's bad side. He's smart but maybe a little dangerous too. After the three of them dispersed we waited another couple of minutes before exiting the tunnel into one of the main corridors.

Only a few lower-class members were left scurrying around. Shawna and I silently went to our rooms. Not sure what to say to each other after overhearing Tyler, Maddy, and Dimitri's conversation.

Are perfect existence, our safe home, and our powerful leader, all seem to be shattered illusions. How could one man whom we looked to as our protector have a prisoner or even have the power to make people disappear? How could he lie to us about the reason behind the alarm? Or why he is holding Quinn prisoner? Who is Quinn? Why do we even live in this Dome if like we learned today the air outside is safe? Well, at least it didn't kill us right away. What mission are Tyler, Dimitri, and Maddy on? What does Lucas have to do with any of this? Why does Dimitri not trust Aki? Isn't he friends and an apprentice with his fellow welder Lucas? All the questions swirling around in my head were giving me a headache. I felt like I was losing my reality. What was even real anymore.....

Chapter 4

My head swirled as I grabbed a quick shower. Not like had much choice in the matter, since we could only shower for 2 minutes, so quick was a bit of an understatement. I hated this thing. It was a slim, Grey tube turned horizontal with barely enough room for me to squeeze into. Let alone turn around or raise my elbows to wash.

In the Dome space was not a luxury that we could not afford to waste. I didn't really consider the ability to turn around in the shower a waste of luxury. It seemed to me to be more of a need, but who was I to say? The Dome was all about sanitation as well. Our shampoo, conditioner, and soap were an all-in-one bright blue variety. It left you smelling more like the infirmary
than anything else. It was not pleasant.
Who likes to think of the infirmary and the needles they give as you are trying to fall asleep? Not the most restful thoughts. But tonight I was willing and grateful to squeeze in the shower tube of small proportions without too much

complaint. That tunnel was nothing less than gross. I am glad it was jet black because from what I see on me now I don't think I could've even entered that nasty old thing if I had known ahead of time! I walked over to the kitchen. The thought of calling it a kitchen made me laugh, not in a funny way but more in irritation. A small sailboat's galley kitchen from former times was 99.9% larger than what the Dome considered to be a kitchen. There was a mini fridge, a small cooktop stove, micro microwave, and a sink. Again all in the glorious Dome Grey. Although, the little sink was a shiny grey metal to mix things up a bit. Don't want the brain getting too bored I guess.

     The Dome was generous if that was what you wanted to call it because we had two cabinets instead of just one. We receive monthly rations for breakfast and snacks. We all ate lunch and dinner in the Center of the Dome. It was the best part. It had a grand garden, bridge, little river, and walking path. There was also a track to run to help us all stay in shape.
The dining hall was open to the green
area which offered a welcomed reprieve from all

the gray. It also had a lounge area with couches and ping-pong tables which we often used in the evenings. I sat down on my little chair at the table in the living room/bedroom area.
There was no clear distinction between the beginning or end of either room. I began eating a package of brownies. One of my favorites. I didn't
remember much else as far as food that didn't come from a package. I have little pieces of memories at times of my mom and dad telling me to try something and then I would like it. But I can't really remember what it was exactly that I was supposed to like. Leaving me to wonder, do I like food that doesn't come in packages? I look around my room with a new light, no longer seeing my quarters as a safe place. Now I understand Tyler's words about our rooms. The cooler he called it. It feels frigid and lonely. I wish Shawna was here. But there is only one person allowed per room.

That does make a lot of sense. There's barely enough room for my small gray bed that I outgrew it two years ago. I was promised a new one but it still hasn't come. You learn not to hold your breath for things here in the Dome. If you did you would died a million times over and that's not an exaggeration. Remember, brains and brawn.

Anyway, I have made a bed on the floor with my one flat pillow. The comforter isn't that bad. It's fluffy and has some weight to it. The cool gray color makes it blend in with all its surroundings. The sheets leave something to be desired. You cannot cover up with them without your Dome uniform. Unless you want to be stabbed to death by a million, yes a million fibers that have long been broken free with the purpose of making your sleep nonexistent. Even when you have a hard time falling asleep, eventually you would from sheer boredom with no view. All that surrounds is gray on top of gray on top of gray. Every room in the Dome except for the Nobles and VI-Count's room, don't have a view.

The higher class is located on the top level of the Dome. They could see for miles. As long as we haven't had a dust storm lately. That would distort their view because of the dust particles settling down on the glass panels. They probably have smooth silky sheets. And I heard they even have couches to sit on instead of a cube-like we get that doesn't even have a back to support us. It was not cool how we were treated so differently. I honestly never really thought of it before now. After I had finished my brownie I sat back with my head against the wall and quickly the morning's excitement caught up with me. I was fast asleep before I could even try to stop myself.

Chapter 5

Slowly, I stirred at first trying to clear the cobwebs from my brain. It's like that with the brainy person in the morning. Got to get the wheels cranked up as it were. It's not easy running at full speed each day. The mind needs a bit of time to recharge. I slept really hard. I knew this because of the pillow being glued to the side of my face by some drool. There's no need to get dressed since you have to sleep in your Dome uniform to survive the sleep-stealing sheets. The gray cargo pants along with the T-shirt topped off with slightly darker gray boots. I almost forgot to mention the grey socks for extra pizzazz.

The uniform is supposed to be tough and withstand our work schedule. Not to be fashionable as Shawna likes to say. I think the undergarments are made from the same angry fabric as the sheets, making it hard to really relax or feel comfortable. Sleeping on a bed of nails is probably more pleasant than the agony we have to go through each day in these torturous clothes. You'd think VI-Count would supply clothing and bedding they were a bit more thoughtful, especially for the amount of work that he expects from us in the Dome.

Suddenly, memories flooded my mind as I reflected on what I do within the Dome. It's me but a much younger version. I'm sitting on the floor with a plastic toy dismantled lying there in front of me. My father was beside me with an intrigued expression on his face. There I am about three years old turning the gears at an agonizingly slow speed of about 3 notches below turtle.

I was so careful not to miss one interlocking of the teeth of the gears. I remember being mesmerized by this simple yet complex routine. Flooding my father with questions as his warm golden-brown eyes watch me with matched curiosity.

He was so patient as I watched his light-colored hands with what seemed to be permanently blackened fingertips explain to me what each gear was doing and what effect it was having on the next.
This probably explains my job here at the Dome. It came naturally to me. I have always had

a deep understanding of how machines work and function. Almost as good as my father but, at a much younger age and without the experience he had. I must've been some type of prodigy for mechanics if there was such a thing. I could listen to how something was running and determine what it needed.

If just a tweak or if it needed to be completely replaced. My mom, Stella used to joke with my dad all the time about how they didn't have to buy me toys. I remember her dark complexion and her gentle smile looking at me with her ocean-like blue eyes sparkling with pride. She wasn't upset that I didn't play with toys like the other kids my age. I could see that she was proud. She never corrected me for taking things apart. Inside she encouraged it.
Except for that one time I took apart her immersible blender. She wasn't happy about that. Until I made it a bit better. She said that she was glad that I improved her blender for her and that it never puréed soup better.

This memory of my parents brought tears to my eyes. I felt a longing to see them. As I was sitting there with my thoughts seeing my parents, it felt so real. The scent of my father, he sent of mechanical grease and sweat came back to my mind slowly at first then hit me hard. I felt like I was hit with ten steel beams collapsing from the top of the Dome, the smell from the tunnel the memory, the one that tickled the back of my brain, it was a memory of my dad.

But why would that smell be in the tunnel? Wouldn't the entire tunnel have that aroma of mechanical grease and sweat? Not just that one area. A thought flashed through my mind. Could my father Emmett whom I have not seen in 12 years, the one whom I have thought for all these years as dead, could have been there right in the Dome close to me? Could he be the one who infiltrated the Dome?

That possibility overwhelmed me with so much emotion. I felt an explosion deep in my insides that ran through me. I wasn't sure if I should be angry or frustrated. I mean all along my father has been alive but he wasn't here with me. Or should I be happy at the realization that he is alive? Then a shiver began to run down my spine as I thought of the possibility that VI-Count and the Nobles may have caught him! Now, I'm overtaken by worry for my mom and dad's safety. These thoughts renewed my desire to go along with Shawna's idea to talk to Dimitri, Tyler, and Maddy. I walked a couple of steps over to the kitchen and opened the small cabinet to the right. My breakfast cabinet. I opened up a packaged blueberry muffin, I think. They all look the same. Grey foil. For some reason, they don't even have a label most of the time.

I didn't really take time to chew or notice the flavor because I was out the door and headed towards Shawna's room. I was determined to get to the bottom of this and relieved to tell her that I was in and that she wouldn't have to convince me of your plan.

I guess that's why I didn't notice Lord Byron until I smashed right into him knocking his forehead with mine. We are about the same height although it was much broader than him.

"Ouch, watch where you're going, you lousy kid!" Spat Lord Byron.

"Sorry, I didn't mean to run into you, Lord Byron. I didn't see you there," said Sebastian sheepishly.

"Of course, you didn't! How you can't expect to see anything with your head down to the floor." Said Lord Byron indignantly.

"Right sorry. I'll make sure to keep my head up and watch I'm going from now on your right," said Sebastian reassuringly.

"Where are you going anyway and in such an absent-minded way," questioned Lord Byron.

"To my work assignment!" I said a little too quickly.

"What? Isn't your work assignment at the end of the East Wing this month? Aren't you helping to repair the crane that's continuing to malfunction?" Said Lord Byron with suspicion in his voice.

"Yes, sir it is," I said as he started to realize my flaw.

Shawna's quarters are a little further down the lower-class wing on the south side of the Dome. Not quite in the direction, I needed to be traveling now.

"Then why are you going deeper in the south wing? How do you expect the crane to be repaired if you're going in the wrong direction? Maybe we shouldn't trust you to repair the equipment if you can't even tell what direction to go in," Lord Byron said with a smirk.

"Sorry sir, going east now," I said.

And with that, I headed down the corridor without another word to Lord Byron. Leaving quickly so he could say another word back to me! I wanted to talk to Shawna but I knew it would have to wait. It would look too suspicious if I was a double back down the hall now. I remembered the letter from my parents. They may be watching you. If they were I didn't want there to be any reason to be watched even closer. When I arrived at the crane I pulled out my tools and got to work. It was quiet. No one was here since the crane was under repair. There was a point since there was nothing anyone could do. There is no way any of us could lift one of the steel beams in place without it. They weighed 1500 lbs.

I was replacing the fuse for the lift mechanism again. This was the third time this month. It's not like the crane to go through so many fuses. I looked, listened, and studied the machine. There was nothing wrong with it! This ordeal had caused me to lose quite a bit of sleep. It wasn't like me to miss something. And it bugged me because I was certain I wasn't missing anything! My brain shifted gears. What if there wasn't anything wrong with the crane? Maybe someone was sabotaging the equipment. That would make sense because I know I cannot be missing anything. It has to be the only explanation. But why? What would anyone gain from sabotaging the Dome's crane? Time but what use would extra time be to anyone? We have nothing but time in the Dome! Why would anyone not want the Dome to be expanded? I wish I could talk to Shawna about this but she was in the North wing.

She worked in laundry. All day long she would wash, dry and iron close with a few other lower-class members. Not that the lower class got their clothes ironed. That's only VI-Count and the Nobles get that kind of treatment. With their comfortable wrinkle-free clothes. She told me they even had to iron their underwear and sheets! Crazy!

There's a lot of laundry since there are 250 people in the Dome. Actually, 251 thanks to the Morris family with their new baby girl Mallory.

Even more unfair is that VI-Count gets to wear a maroon vest. Not that I like maroon vests, but color! It would be nice to have a little color. You could say so much about how you were feeling.

Maybe it was a way for VI-Count to keep us from feeling like individuals. I mean he viewed all the lower class as well, lower. A group of workers without names, interests, wants, just tools. I guess it would be more work for the laundry room to actually have to sort colors. I don't know. The laundry room doesn't need any more work. It's hard and hot.

Shawna is a good sport though. She says it's a dirty job but someone's got to do it or we wouldn't be able to live together under the same roof because of the smell of 251 armpits times two. I was extra grateful after that speech for her services as well.

I was wondering if she got to talk to Tyler, Maddy, or Dimitri. I didn't think so since Dimitri was with Lucas in the West wing finishing up the welding on the crack. And Maddy worked in the kitchen, which was also in the North wing but closer to Central.

Maddy had a different job. She helped feed the 251 hungry mouths that lived in the Dome twice a day. She was grateful that we all had our own breakfast for sure! Although I usually
had a muffin, we also could have a protein bar or packaged protein shake. The protein shakes were more like the consistency of toothpaste with a much less appealing flavor. That's why I usually went for the muffins.

Young ones are required to take a vitamin each day they were supposed to make up for the nutrients and minerals we missed because of our limited diet here in the Dome. I have totally forgotten to take my vitamin the last couple of days. To be honest, I'm feeling better without it, less fuzzy. Not sure why?

For lunch and dinner when we go to the center, we all gather together, listen to announcements, and eat our lunch (Usually some type of potato), then we will return for dinner to hear any updates or goings-on of the day. Again potatoes that may be spiced up a bit with some beans.

Food's grown in the Dome. But it's limited.

We had a lot of potatoes, beans, and beets. We also had cucumbers, spinach, lettuce, and similar items but they had to be consumed to a lesser degree.

We do not have any animals here in the Dome. Since air and life outside of the Dome were supposedly not safe, no one traveled out to try to hunt. Oh boy, did I do I ever miss the meat. I loved hamburgers, chicken nuggets, chicken tenders, bacon, and sausage. Did I say bacon? I needed to stop thinking about this the thoughts alone are making me drool.

One of the reasons for the expansion was so that we could have a larger garden area to grow more food and different varieties. VI-Count is said to have different types of seeds from life before the Dome so that we can have more to choose from and be able to feed the growing number. I sure hope he has some bacon seeds or at least some chocolate. There's a plant here that is supposed to taste like chocolate but it doesn't. Not at all! There just isn't a substitute for a good old-fashioned chocolate bar. Drooling again. Tyler works in the greenhouse. He helps with the planting and harvesting. They probably picked him for the job because there's a lot of going up and down the rows along with bending, and heavy lifting during the harvest. That's also probably another reason he's so in shape and sporty.

The lower class liked to play basketball. Every year Tyler was on the All-Star team. He also runs track. It's a decent workout running around the center a couple of times. But I never could hang with Tyler he is a beast when it comes to running. He beats most of the adults even with the

exception of Lucas.

When I finished up changing the fuse and placing all the paneling back in place I spotted something out of the corner of my eye. It was shoved down between the two hydraulic lifts. I crammed my arm down in a space normally it would never fit. I gritted my teeth and tried to ignore the pain. It felt like my flesh was being shredded by the various bolts I was pushing past. I almost had it.

My fingers kept brushing past it. Come on I said to myself. I was so close. My arm was starting to tingle from the lack of blood flow from the tight quarters. Finally, when I felt like I would not be able to take anymore, my middle and pointer fingers close together with the paper between them. I gingerly as possible pulled out the paper while holding my breath afraid to have gone through all that just to let it slip away. Greasy fingerprints were on the outside of the paper. I could tell they were not mine because it was dried and flaky. Different from the fresh moist grease that I had just smeared.

I looked around cautiously the letter burning between my fingers like it might explode any minute. I quickly put it into my pocket realizing my idea that the crane is being purposely sabotaged is the answer. I was wondering if VI-Count or the Nobles might have the same idea and be watching me. I had to wait until I went back to my room before I could see what it said. My stomach was in a knot. I wanted to know but at the same time, I was not so sure that I really did. I felt like everyone was watching me. It's weird how that happens. When you have a secret it feels as if everyone can peer inside you and see what you are thinking. I shivered at the thought.

Chapter 6

Before I could go to dinner I would have to go back to my room and wash up. I am so hungry by this point in the day I almost forget the letter. I reached into my pocket and pulled the note out so gingerly, as if it may crumble in my hands. Eager but afraid to see what it contained inside. I started to open but stopped. Someone was rapidly knocking on my door. I quickly stuff to letter back into my uniform pants and open the door. It's Shawna. I let her in and breathed a sigh of relief.

"What's wrong Sebastian you look terrible. Was it your work assignment? Are you still not sleeping well because of the crane?" Questioned Shawna rapidly with deep concern in her voice.

This was a custom of Shawna's. Sometimes I would get lost in which question to answer first, but not this time. My adrenaline was running so rapidly through my body but it almost seemed like she was talking in slow motion from my perspective. But a simple yes and no was not what was needed to really explain.

"Yes and No. I'm not sure where to begin..." I said slightly confused.

"Just start talking. That might work you Lugnut," said Shawna soothingly.

Shawna affectionately calls me this when she knows I am upset and is trying to calm me down a few notches. It was a pet name my parents had for me when I was little. It's a nut that goes on the thread that holds a tire in place on a vehicle that we used to drive around called cars and trucks before we came into the doom and those types of transportation became obsolete. Well I didn't drive them I was too young, but my parents did.

I start to recount to Shawna my thoughts about the crane and how I think it's been purposely sabotaged the last three weeks. It's the only solution I can come up with. Shawna was listening intently nodding every now and then. She seemed to be drinking up every word I said as her light brown eyes were laser-focused on me. I noticed her hair was a bit messier than normal and her eyes had deep dark circles darker even than her skin. I started to wonder if she got any sleep last night. Here she was trying to calm me down but she looked like she needed a bit of peace herself. No sooner had I finished my thoughts when Shawna began to speak.

"Is there anything else?" She asked worriedly

"Like what," I asked a little thrown back.

I mean she can't know about the letter. How could she? I thought to myself.

"No," I said uneasily.

Wasn't sure what to say. It could be nothing I might just be paranoid from
everything that has been going on the last few days. I didn't want to doubt my best friend or even think she was capable of spying on me. I quickly shook those thoughts out of my mind. Then I was blown away by what Shawna said next!

"Didn't you find a piece of paper?" Shawna asked me slowly.

"How did you know that? I was alone!" I said stunned.

My mind began to whirl. No, no, not Shawna too. Today has been crazy enough, I could not handle my best friend being in on whatever it was that was going on.

"Because I found one too," said Shawna with a hint of fear in her voice.

A mixture of relief and fear tangled together. Leaving my facial expression a bit odd and unable to read. I could tell because Shawna gave me a very strange like that said, dude what is wrong with your face? After my face relaxed into a more suitable facial expression for the situation, we just looked at each other in amazement unsure what to do next. Concern etched in both of our brows. My heart was racing. Both of us received a letter. What was this about? What did they say?

Chapter 7

I slowly pulled the note from my pocket and opened it. Shawna and I bumped heads as we both leaned in to peer over the words.

"Ouch," Shawna said as she pulled back rubbing her forehead.

"Sorry," I said quickly.

```
LUGNUT,

STOP FIXING THE CRANE!
```

That was it. Right there in front of me. Proof! There really wasn't anything wrong with the crane! With the name Lugnut, I knew it was from my mom and dad. Meaning they could be the ones behind the crane sabotaging.

Shawna's voice brought me back into the present.

"Lugnut. That's what you told me your parents called you when you were young," said Shawna surprised.

"It was," I said solemnly.

"But why would your parents want to sabotage the crane? Don't they know VI-Count is opening up the Dome so that we can have different types of food and be able to feed the growing population?" Said Shawna in an accusing tone.

Couldn't blame her for using that kind of tone. She wasn't alone we all longed for something other than potatoes! And the thought that my parents might be behind this leads to so many unanswered questions. Something that we definitely had plenty of. We haven't seen our parents in over 12 years. How do we know that we can even trust them? If they really cared about our safety wouldn't they be here with us now? Confusion was clouding my judgment and thoughts.

"Wait!" Shawna almost shouted

"What if VI-Count isn't being honest? I mean it does seem like we can't trust him any longer doesn't it? What if the expansion of the Doom doesn't have anything to do with being able to grow more food or for the growth of a population? What if there's some other intention or plan?" Questioned Shawna.

"Do you think he might be planning something else for the expansion, other than food? There go to my bacon seeds in chocolate!" I said disappointedly

"Maybe, I'm not sure. To be honest I'm not sure of anything anymore. I used to feel like I had it all figured out and in control. But now I feel a bit lost. I'm not totally comfortable with that idea of not knowing." Said Shawna miserably.

For a long moment, we just sat there allowing our spinning minds to slow. After a few moments, I noticed a piece of paper being held by Shawna's slender fingers. She noticed me looking down at her dark hand and spoke.

"I totally forgot. I found this in my pants pocket. The weird part is that they were cleaned three days ago. I just hadn't had a chance to take them back to my room with all the confusion, and then the lockdown. I spotted a corner peeking out of my pants pocket. It was impossible though because I always check and clean my pockets out before I wash them. And this paper was undamaged. So I couldn't have missed it before the wash. It was put in after." Shawna said slowly and quietly.

Almost afraid to say her thoughts out loud.

"Did you read it?" I asked timidly. Equally afraid.

"No, not yet. I was a little afraid. With all that happened last night and then with the lockdown yesterday. Knowing someone may be in the Dome. After already receiving the letter from our parents the day before. I wasn't sure I even wanted to know what this one says. I didn't want to open it alone," said Shawna in a small voice, one I had never heard her use before.

She was really shaken up. It was so evident by the frazzled expression on her face. I could see the fear in her eyes and the worry in her brow. Her lips loose almost trembling. I gave her a hug and told her that everything was gonna be OK. We were going to get through this together. Determined to figure this out and protect my best friend I knew we had to read Shawna's letter and continue to move forward. Not allowing the unknown or fear to paralyze us from acting. I also felt a pang of guilt for ever doubting Shawna's loyalty or intention. I would not make that mistake again.

"Well, there's only one way for us to find out what we need to do next. We have to read the letter. It'll be OK I'm right here and we're gonna get through this together." I said as firmly and reassuringly as I possibly could.

TIGRIS,
WE NEED FOUR UNIFORMS.
ADULT SIZE. LEAVE THEM IN THE
CORNER UNDER THE OVERHANG NEAR
THE REPAIRS SITE TONIGHT.
BE CAREFUL THAT YOU WERE NOT
FOLLOWED!

"Tigris? Who in the world is Tigres?" I asked perplexed.

"I haven't been called Tigres since the last time I had seen my parents. My mom and dad called me Tigris because I was so feisty. I also liked to crawl around on all four legs and roar like a tiger," said Shawna mournfully followed by a brief chuckle from the memory.

I let out a small laugh as well. I was cracked up by the thought of a small Shawna crawling around on the floor roaring like a big bad tiger. Fear was not the emotion that came to mind. Shawna had a far-off look in her light brown eyes. I could tell that she was there with her parents, as their little Tigris, safe in their company. As I was observing her I noticed a small tear forming in her now sad-looking eyes. Her hair as usual was all over the place. A mixture of her mom's loose wavy curls and her dad's tight curls. Leaving her hair unsure of what to do.

Some days it really had a mind of its own. Shawna once told me that she wished her mom was here to help her know how to tame what she found to be uncontrollable. Her dark complexion turned even darker in an instant. Her eyes furrowed as she looked up at me with sudden determination.

"Sebastian, do you remember anything about the last time you saw your parents? Or even why you were taken? Or when?" Shawna asked with a blazing intensity that kind of frightened me.

"I had my first memory earlier today. It was the clearest memory I've had that I can remember in the Dome. But other than that I just have an unsettled feeling about it and unclear memories." I said sadly.

"I just had an odd memory. One where my parents were fighting with a man. They were shouting and yelling. I heard my mom say that they would never be able to take Shawna. And my dad was frantic after the men had left. I overheard them saying that we had to get away so that they would never find us. Or more importantly me. A moment later the lights went out in the home and someone put a hand over my mouth and pulled me away from my mom and dad. For days I was locked away alone and afraid. I couldn't tell where I was because I had a cover over my eyes. Everything seemed so dark and cold. There was constant movement. I knew I was being taken somewhere but not sure where. But I did know it meant that I wouldn't see my parents again. I promised myself if I ever got through that I would never allow anyone to make me feel so small again." Shawna said coldly.

"How are you remembering all this? I have no clear memories of life before the Dome." I asked Shawna intrigued

Chapter 8

"How are you able to remember all of that?" I repeated astonished.

"I have a theory. Not sure if you will believe me. Not really sure if I believe it myself," said Shawna with uncertainty clearly seen on her face.

"Like I said I was sick and I couldn't keep anything down for a couple of days. I didn't even try to take my vitamin. Ever since then, it's like you said, I feel less cloudy, I feel more like my old self. It's strange because I don't remember really feeling like myself completely since life outside of the Dome. I just chalked it up to missing my parents maybe. Along with never being able to go outside. But in honesty, I don't really miss them. I reflected on this for a while. And that just wasn't normal. If I lost you I would be devastated. Shouldn't I be even more upset by the loss of my own parents?" Said, Shawna deep concern pouring out of every syllable.

"I get what you mean I had the same lack of grief too. It's weird now that you mention it. I never really thought about it." I said disappointed in myself.

"That's just it Lugnut. I think it's the 'vitamins' that are making us feel this way. Now that it has been a week since I haven't taken mine I'm remembering more and more. Like that huge memory of the night I was taken!" Said Shawna excitedly.

I pondered on this for a while. It seems to be wrong on so many levels. Not just the fact that VI-Count ripped us away from our parents. But brainwashing us of our grief and attachment to our parents. That's crazy! Only a madman could be behind something so truly diabolical. What purpose is there for a man who claims to be our protector to abduct us from our own parents and then make us forget them? I feel like I have been robbed of 12 years of memories and feelings.

"It's so unfair!" I angrily said out loud unknowingly.

"That's the understatement of the century!" exclaimed Shawna.

"Well, I can guarantee you that I will not be taking my 'vitamins' from now on!" I said matter-of-factly.

"Agreed!" Said Shawna with conviction.

"Wait, wait," I said quickly.

"What is it?" Shawna said with concern.

"Once a year we get a shot, what is it supposed to be for?" I questioned.

Shawna thought for a moment then added. "You know that's a good question. I totally forgot about the shot. I remember them saying it's a high-dose immune booster that's supposed to help us fight off disease since we live in tight quarters with so many others,"

"I have a sneaking suspicion that the 'vitamins' are the only booster needed to carry the effects of the shot for a longer period of time," I say conclusively.

"That makes perfect sense!" Agreed Shawna.

"Well, we need to not take our 'vitamins' to start with, as well as steer clear from the infirmary. Maxine and Logan might get suspicious if we don't show up for our shot though. When are we doing for the next one," asked Shawna.

"I think we are definitely due for one in the next couple of weeks," said Shawna wearily.

I could understand her concern. I felt the

same. That little memory was huge for me. I didn't want to lose the connection I was starting to get back with my parents. I wonder if I would have a memory of the day when I was taken from my parents soon like Shawna. Not that I was eager.

I wanted to know but at the same time, it's been really hard on Shawna. It's almost too much to handle. To learn so much of your life was a lie so quickly. I feel so fragile like an old window pane that with the slightest breath it would shatter. Where are we going to get the strength to be able to handle all of this?
I turned to Shawna who was in a deflated-looking pose, head down, shoulder slumped. Her hands hugged against her knees. I can see a tear glistening on her face as a cascaded down her cheek onto the floor. Leaving a wet spot on the note that lay beside her.

"Shawna, Tigris, we can do this. We have each other. We have our parents. They're alive. Somewhere. We are not alone. We need to go and talk to Tyler, Maddy, and Dimitri. We need to know what they know. We need all the info that we can get." I said as confidently as possible with my back straightened, my head held high. Trying to convince myself that we were gonna be ok just as much as I was trying to convince Shawna.

"What about the four adult uniforms?" asked Shawna.

"That's right I almost forgot! Yes, we can do that together after dinner. I will take a sack of dirty laundry down and you can give me the 'fresh' clothes. Then we could take that nasty tunnel to the damaged site and make the deposit. Mission accomplished!" I said confidently just as much for Shawna as myself.

"I like your pessimism but something tells me it might not work out so well," said Shawna.

Chapter 9

As we made our way to the north wing we tried to come up with ways to start a conversation with Tyler, Maddy, and Dimitri. Shawna was convinced that we should not even make eye contact with Tyler. I was apt to agree since I had seen firsthand how he treated his friends. I was thinking Maddy, and Shawna was thinking Dimitri. Anyone but Tyler.

How are we going to do this? Just go up to them and say, hey don't take your vitamins or get your shot they're really brainwashing tools so you don't remember your parents. By the way, they might be alive. VI-Count has lied about the plans to

expand the Dome and feed us something other than potatoes it's also a lie. How are you going to go and shatter someone else's illusion like that? What if they couldn't handle it? What if they told on us? Can we even trust them? Oh yeah, did I mention someone is sabotaging the crane and Quinn is being held prisoner by VI-Count? Shawna, did I miss anything? No, I think you covered it. The conversation in my mind was consuming me so I barely felt Shawna grab me by the shoulder for the third time and whisper in my ear. "There they are in the back left corner."

Well, as back left corner as you could be in a circular room. We started to walk over. I noticed an odd look from Lucas. I found that strange. Shouldn't be happy that the unions are making friends?

"Hey," Shawna said all nonchalant-like.

Making it seem like we talked to the three of them all the time.

"Hey!" said Maddy politely in return.

"Hey yourself!" Spat Tyler.

"Don't mind him." Said Dimitri timidly.

A thought crossed my mind. They seemed as nervous as we were. All except for Tyler. Why do they seem so nervous? Maddy scooted over to make room for Shawna and Dimitri slid over to make room for me. Tyler well, he's Tyler so he didn't move a muscle.

"How are you all doing?" Shawna said casually.

"Cut the small talk, Shawna! You never talk to us or even look our way. What do you want?" Said Tyler indignantly.

"Don't be so rude!" Said Maddy defensively.

"It's OK Maddy. He's right. Sorry to say. To be honest I'm not even sure why we haven't talked or hung out. I'm not gonna pretend it's any different." Said Shawna honestly.

"It's not all on you." Said Dimitri quickly.

"What do you mean?" I asked curiously.

"We were told to stay away from you and Sebastian." Said, Maddy

"By who? And Why?" Ask Shawna with the storm cloud breaming in her eyes.

"What are you two doing? Why are you trusting them? Remember what we were told" Questioned Tyler angrily.

"What's going on?" Shawna asked impatiently.

They didn't know Shawna like me if someone did not start explaining themselves Shawna was going to lose it! I wasn't even sure how long she could take it now that she's off her 'vitamins'. Shawna was feisty before, if that was her as calm feisty, I don't know what she would be capable of without the calm portion!

"We know that Quinn is being held prisoner by VI-Count!" I said quickly.

Tyler, Maddy, and Dimitri all shot straight up. They quickly sat back down not trying to draw attention to themselves. I seem to have gotten their attention

"How do you know that? Who told you?" Demanded Tyler outraged.

"It's hard to explain," I said calmly.

"Cut the excuses and start talking!" Fumed Tyler.

Who does this jerk think he is, Shawna held me back from lunging toward him!

"You might want to share it with us." Said Maddy in a calming tone.

"How do we know that we can trust you?" I asked.

"OK, look Lucas told us to stay away from you. He said you both might be under surveillance, and that would make things murky for us." Said Dimitri in barely a whisper.

"Now tell us how you know about Quinn?" Demanded Tyler.

"We got a note?" I said.

"A note, from who?" Demanded Tyler.

"We found it on the floor by the creak," said Shawna.

They all looked at each other puzzled.

"Did you miss a communication, Maddy?" Tyler was furious with her.

"I didn't miss anything! Drop it!" Retorted Maddy.

"No, it was for us. We know this for sure because it had our names on it." I said

"Your names for real?" Asked Dimitri intrigued.

"Yes!" I said firmly.

I finally felt like we were starting to get someone. At least Tyler wasn't demanding things at the moment, which was good. I have had all the demands from him that I could handle for the day!

"What did it say? If you don't mind sharing," asked Maddy genuinely interested.

"It said 'Shawna, and Sebastian, we need your help. VI-Count has lied to us all. He has captured Quinn. Be careful he may be watching you both! Love you Sebastian Mom and Dad Shawna, we love you Mom and Dad" I said slowly and deliberately careful not to miss anything while watching their faces turn from disbelief into intrigue.

"Wow, that's deep." Said Tyler stunned.

"We have never gotten a message from my parents." Said Maddy with deep sadness in her voice.

"Sorry to hear that Maddy, sorry for all of you," I said soothingly and I meant it.

"I am not even sure if our parents are alive." Said Dimitri in an even sadder tone and Maddy.

This was breaking my heart.

"Lucas never told us that any of our parents were alive or dead. We just assumed they were since we never dared to hope." Said Maddy reflectively.

"We were shocked about it as well. We had no idea that they were alive. For the last 12 years, we thought they were dead. I mean what other reason would there be for them not to be here with us." I explained

"What are their names?" Asked Dimitri curiously.

"My mother's name is Maya and my father's Malcolm." said, Shawna.

"I have heard Quinn talk about Maya. He said you don't want to get on her bad side. She's awfully feisty. He said she can be a bit overconfident at times which has led to a couple of setbacks to our mission." Said, Maddy

"What Mission?" I asked.

"We don't know much right now other than to stall the expansion of the Dome as long as possible is there a key objective at the moment." Said Dimitri.

"Were any of you responsible for the fuse in the crane?" I asked already knowing the answer was no.

"What do you mean?" Asked Dimitri intrigued.

"The fuse has been blown out three different times, but there's no reason for it," I said with complete confidence.

"No that wasn't us." Said Tyler.

Seem to be a bit upset that he thought about something like sabotaging the crane.

"I didn't think it was. I mean I found note stuff down inside next to the hydraulic levers." I said.

"Who do you think left the note?" Maddy asked.

"I know it was for my dad. It had his blackened fingerprints all over it and it said to not let the crane get up and running." I said clearly.

"What are your parent's names, Sebastian?" Asked Maddy curiously.

"My mother is Stella and my father is Emmett," I said proudly.

It was nice to talk about them even if it was just to say their name.

"No way! Your father is Emmett, the man is someone who skills, I dream of. He can just listen to a machine and know what's wrong with it. VI-Count wanted him so bad and when he refused to join him, VI-Count promised to ruin his life. Man, your father is truly a master mine." Beemed Dimitri with such awe and admiration that made my chest unknowingly puff up a bit more with pride.

"I can do that too. That's how I knew there was nothing wrong with the crane in the first place." I said probably.

"Are you for real? Man, I am so jealous of you and your dad!" Whined Dimitri.

"Will you gear slingers get a grip? We have more important matters to discuss other than listening to machines!" demanded Tyler, breaking up the bit of happiness that they had for the first time today.

"One more thing," Shawna added. "I also received a note."

Chapter 10

"You got a note too!" Exclaimed Tyler with what seemed to be a note of jealousy in his voice.

"Keep your voice down, someone I might hear you," whispered shouted Maddy.

Dimitri unlike Tyler was not led by his emotions and therefore was the next speaker getting the conversation back on target.

"What did your note say?" Dimitri asked gently.

"We need four uniforms, adult size. Leave them in the corner under the overhang near the repair site tonight. Be careful that you are not followed," recited Shawna, as diligently as I was careful not to leave one word out.

"That could be from anyone," said Tyler still emotionally charged.

I was beginning to think that this was his regular state. Always in an emotional upheaval about something. That's probably why they have him run up and down the isles all day to try to tire him out so no one has to listen to his complaining or ranting. I was about to suggest to Tyler that maybe he should take a hike when Maddy spoke.

"It could be a trap or setup of some kind," Maddy agreed.

"It is not a setup or a trap I can assure you," Shawna said with confidence.

"I have seen the note it was definitely for Shawna," I said doing my best to back my best friend up.

She gave me a small smile that seemed to say thank you. I did my best to send a facial expression back that said no problem but I am not sure what my face did because she looked at me a bit oddly for a moment. I could see why Shawna left out the "Tigris
 part. I mean I didn't mention"Lugnut" and I am sure that Shawna was trying to avoid her parent's pet name from being revealed. It's one thing for your parents to call you something but it is another for your friends to get a hold of it. Who knows what might happen then? Especially Tyler! I didn't see Maddy or Dimitri being a problem though.

"How do you know for sure that this isn't a trap?" asked Dimitri calmly but in a matter-of-fact kind of way.

"Because it was from my parents. They wrote a name on the note, one that they called me. One which only they will ever call me." Shawna said firmly with an I dare you to ask kind of look.

I think everyone got the picture, even Tyler. I think Shawna might kind of scare Tyler. Shawna kind of scares me sometimes and I know her the best.

"OK, so we know both of your parents must be in the Dome since they are asking for four adult uniforms," said Maddy.

"They were not supposed to start coming in until the uprising was complete," said Dimitri to himself.

"What uprising?" asked Shawna

"It's the purpose of our mission. To help prepare for the uprising," said Maddy.

"I guess we have no choice but to trust you and to tell you everything! We are supposed to slow the construction project as we said. But we are also supposed to gather supplies." said Tyler gravely.

This was the first hint of a serious emotionally stable person inside that whirlwind of a boy, Tyler. He seemed torn though at the thought of letting Shawna and me in on all the details.

"What kind of supplies?" Shawna quickly chimed in and asked.

"Food packets, flashlights, extra clothes, first aid kits, water, you know the essentials," listed Maddy.

"Why all that stuff?" I questioned.

"You two really don't know much, do you?" asked Tyler, reverting back to the shallow person we all know and can't stand.

His green eyes filled with indignation, his laid-back posture replaced by one that was rigid and defensive.

"Stop Tyler! They wouldn't have heard Lucas' stories about life outside the Dome." Maddy said defensively.

Her brown eyes seemed to plead with Tyler to chill and let his guard down a bit. I felt as though Maddy really trusted us, which made me relax a little.

"You would be just as lost Tyler if it wasn't for

Lucas. So cut him some slack!" retorted Dimitri.

"Life outside the Dome isn't an easy one. The remaining outsiders have to live underground so as not to be spotted by the Corp." Said Dimitri solemnly.

His shoulders drooped as he seemed to be lost in his mind reflecting on the many stories that Lucas had told them about how the ones on the outside are struggling and are in need of our help. These thoughts seemed to fuel an inner strength in Dimitri. One I had never seen from him before.

"What happens if you get caught," I asked with a tremble in my voice that I could not hide.

Face it, I was more than a little afraid.

"The Watchman turns anyone that is caught over to VI-Count. They are not to be messed with. To call them massive would be an understatement," said Maddy gravely.

"No joking, I think VI-Count has a secret lab under the Dome where he genetically engineers the Watchman. Because there is no way a person could be naturally that large. And come on, how do you find so many square-jawed people with a buzz cut? As I said, it's unnatural and it's weird.

they wore gray uniforms, but they mix it up a bit with a maroon hat and vest for good measure I guess," said Tyler shivering from the memory.

"Brutus is the worst of them all. That guy has no heart or remorse! He is the largest of the Watchman with his cold black eyes and jet back hair that is slicked back with a gallon of grease." Maddy said coldly.

"Hank isn't too far behind with his lifeless steel grey eyes. I heard he turned his own mother over to VI-Count. No one ever heard from her again," added Dimitri.

"What kind of monsters ate these people!" I exclaimed.

"Ones we need to avoid at all costs!" Maddy said with all seriousness.

"Danny is the smallest but he is no joke. That guy can bend a steal bar with his bare hands. He probably eats nailed for breakfast. He is not very bright though. He follows Brutus and Hank around. He probably would get lost going to his own quarters if he was forced to think on his own," Tyler added with a laugh.

Although I could not see how this was at all a laughing matter! I could attest to the size. I am muscular myself, but they make me seem like a pipsqueak in comparison. The thought that Shawna's parents as well as my own had to live these dangerous lives, hiding out underground made me almost happy to live in the Dome. At least we have sunlight, food, and clothes, and we can move around freely. Well, as freely as possible in a bubble.

"Who is this Tobey we keep hearing about?" asked Shawna blurted out, forgetting that it was from Tyler, Maddy, and Dimitri's conversation that we overheard while we were in the tunnel.

I quickly shot Shawna a look and tensed hoping they wouldn't ask how it was that we knew about Tobey. And to my relief, they didn't. I relaxed and let out a sigh. I think they were all so caught up in the conversation that they didn't even think about how we would've heard about Tobey. Or they could have been distracted by the fact that Lucas was now standing over my shoulder. I gulped and looked up. Under normal circumstances, I would've welcomed to visit Lucas, but this time was a lot different. Especially since he told Tyler, Dimitri, and Maddy to stay away from us so that we did not compromise the mission. Tyler was the first to break the silence.

"Hey, Lucas!" Tyler said as nonchalantly as Shawna did when we first approached.

"Hello, Children," Lucas said coldly.

"Nice to see you all together," he said, sarcasm dripping from his voice.

"Hey, Shawna and Sebastian don't you have somewhere to be?" Questioned Lucas.

He had an urgency in his voice as he looked down at his watch. Yikes, dinner had been over for 30 minutes and we were almost the last ones left in the Center. We had to go make the drop. But wait, how could Lucas know about the drop? Or was he just saying that to get rid of us? I wasn't sure until I looked directly at him, making eye contact. I knew at once that he knew. The truth was in his eyes. Shawn and I gathered the sack of dirty clothes ready to carry out the mission for our parents, it was our mission. We left without even looking back. Tyler Maddy and Dimitri already knew where we were headed so there was no need for goodbyes.

Chapter 11

Shawna and I left the Center. We did not dare to speak. So much had been discussed. So much to process. I would love nothing more than to sit and talk about what we learned. But we didn't have time. We had to get the uniforms to our parents, without being followed or caught. It's ironic how you could be followed for hours and not even be aware. But when you think that you could be followed, now everyone becomes a suspect, every nook or cranny is a place for someone to hide.

I felt like cameras were everywhere and bugs could pick up any and every sound you made. The mind plays such evil tricks as paranoia mounts. It makes you feel a bit crazy. I could not take much more of this. I was starting to spiral in my mind. Suddenly, I plowed into the folding table in the laundry room. I had been so lost in my mind and the possibilities that I didn't even notice how far we had traveled from the Center up the North wing to laundry. Even passing the kitchen.

Which by now would have the lingering smell of sanitizer as the kitchen crew cleaned up for the night. Yikes! I thought to myself, am I like a beacon for the Watchman? They probably are like "Hey, get a load of this kid, we can walk right up next to him eating a brownie and he wouldn't see us or hear us." Brownie, I must be hungry again. All of this sneaking around and fear must really be burning calories.

"Are you all right?" Shawna asked slightly annoyed.

It's not my fault that I am bleeding again. I mean the gash on my head was complements of hers truly. This one was probably my fault though, but I'm not totally clear. Shawna groaned and muttered something to herself. I think it was something like, why does he have to be so oblivious and clumsy? I tried not to take offense, I mean I know my timing was not the best. I started to say I was sorry but She just cut me a look. Her light brown eyes narrowed to mere slits. This is a look that I know all too well. 'Be quiet, I do not need any excuses!' Quickly, Shawna grabbed the first aid kit from the far wall. She dug around in the kit until she found what she was looking for then went to work cleaning the wound. It was a lot deeper than I thought because she told me she would have to give me a couple of stitches.

"Stitches!" I yelped. Starting to panic. I hate did I say hate, hate, hate needles! Don't laugh there are a lot of tough guys out there that curl up into a ball and whimper a bit at the idea. So I am totally normal in my response. I was going to attempt to explain to Shawna my thoughts but she cut me off.

"Be quiet you big baby! You do not want the entire Dome to hear you, do you?" questioned Shawna.

Totally lacking compassion. I thought of Hank and how heartless he was to turn his own mother in. Well, in this moment there was a bit too much of a resemblance between Hank and Shawna. More than I would like to admit.

"Have you ever given anyone stitches before?" I asked not really sure that I wanted to hear the answer.

"Well, no not until now. It can't be that hard though. Probably similar to sewing up a busted seam, which I do all the time." Shawna said confidently.

"I am not a pair of pants or a shirt!" I exclaimed offended.

"Just breathe! I got this!" Shawna spoke reassuringly then before I could protest or stall any longer she went to work.

I put my head back and tried to obey. Breathing didn't seem to be an option at the moment though. It was more like holding your breath and clenching your fists and teeth so as not to scream. I was clenching so hard I felt like my teeth were going to shatter and fall out right there on the laundry room floor. I was feeling a bit dizzy from holding my breath. I had to take Shawna's advice and breathe, but how? I tried to will my mind to think of something else. I looked at the ceiling. Yuck, I was disgusted by what I saw. It was so soiled. Not a nice bright white color like the Center or any other place in the Dome. I could be wrong though. I haven't been in each room so I have the opportunity to look up and inspect the ceilings. They all might be just as bad. I guess the years of solvents ate away at the paint. I thought of my friend, and the damage to her lungs, as well as her skin, and I shuddered at the thought. This was not a helpful exercise. I was searching for a different angle when I spotted something. I would've never seen it if I was not lying on my back while Shawna was busy putting stitches into my thigh. Now that the pain was more of a throb I returned my eyes to Shawna.

"How bad is it Doc?" I questioned.

"Not too bad. Only 5 stitches," Shawna replied.

She seemed relieved to be done. It could not have been easy for her, could it? Knowing Shawna I was said to think that she probably enjoyed it. Payback for all the stupid things I said and did throughout the years. No that's not right. Shawna's not like that at all. I was beginning to question myself as to whether or not I should be trusting my thinking. First, I wasn't sure if I was delirious from the pain or if I really did see it. I muttered a quick thanks. I wasn't sure if it was audible though, until she responded.

"Don't mention it. But can we keep the blood in your body from now on?" She said in a serious tone.

"I'll try my best." was my lame response.

My mind was still stuck on the little concave Dome hidden mostly by the huge ceiling vent fan. I leaned forward pulling my pant leg down while whispering to Shawna.

"Have you ever noticed that camera up next to the rusty vent fan overhead?" I asked quietly.

Shawna began to raise her eyes to look up but I quickly told her to keep her eyes down and not to draw attention to it.

"No, I have never seen it here before," she said so sure of herself.

"Remember, the note they may be watching you, be careful that you are not followed," I recited.

"Great, that must be new. But somehow our parents knew about it," Shawna said, deep in thought.

"How are we going to get the uniforms without being seen?" I asked puzzled.

"I have an idea," said Shawna.

She ran over to the clean laundry bin and reached deep down inside for a few moments. Later, she told me to take off my pants. She handed me a fresh pair but when I tried to put them on it was a little tricky. I noticed she had put two pairs of pants together. She's a genius. Then two shirts. You couldn't even tell. OK, so that was two uniforms down.

Shawna made a big show of pointing to my pants and shirt. Showing me the bloodstains and applying pre-treatment chemicals. That way they would come out. As she was walking towards the industrial-size washer she tripped and the clothes flew into the clean adult uniform pile that overflowed out for their container. Quickly she pulled the same maneuver switching out the dirty for the clean. It was easy for her to do this maneuver in secret due to the large size of
these containers. We could easily fit inside with room for two more.

Then she set the clothes down by the washer. She told me to bring over my dirty clothes and made a show of telling me what she was going to do. She even sprayed some crazy strong blue chemical cleaner which immediately had me questioning where anyone should really do doing this job. Then she had me stand in a way so as to block as much of her as possible from the view of the camera. She took the dirty

clothes out and slid the clean clothes into the bag,
the adult uniforms.

I was grateful for the first time that all of our clothes were gray. This made Shawna's maneuvers even more seamless!
She shoved them into the bottom of the laundry sack. You would have thought that she had practiced this a million times! I barely saw what she was doing even though I was watching and knew that she was up to something. Now that we had the uniforms we were headed from my least favorite place. The smelly pitch-black tunnel with who knows what from who knows where.

Chapter 12

As we worked our way back down towards the Center we were more aware of the possibilities of new cameras. Neither of us had ever seen cameras in the Dome until today when we had seen the one in the laundry room. What our parents have asked us to do seemed even more dangerous than before. It made me think if our parents are willing to put us in so much danger then what would be the outcome if we failed? Dimitri said life outside the Dome was difficult, so much so that anyone outside the Dome had to live underground and be on guard careful not to be spotted by the Watchman. And the provisions Maddy had mentioned made me wonder, how they have been able to survive for so long. These were basic items that we needed for everyday survival!

Everything is provided for us here. We have food, water, clothes, shelter. We don't even have crime. I mean, I thought we didn't have crime until today. Maddy, Tyler, and Dimitri are stealing from the Dome and now Shawna and I are

stealing too. VI-Count has a prisoner, so I guess things aren't as safe as I thought. I wonder how the people on the outside function.
How did they get water? How did they eat?
I knew they had to live underground but that was the extent of my knowledge. I was hoping to be able to talk to my parents but the idea was overwhelming. I hadn't seen them for so long. Would I even recognize them, or would they even recognize me?

As we entered into the tunnel of black disgustingness. I was more aware of just how nasty the tunnel was. Thick dark grease covered the walls. Not really sure what it was exactly. Maybe years of grease buildup from the kitchen vents that poured into the tunnel. Shawna and I were careful not to get the uniforms dirty as I took the two uniforms I had placed over the top of mine off. She shoved them into the bag. Without a word, Shawna tied the bag uptight as we were coming close to the end of the tunnel.
Shawna halted abruptly in front of me at the sound of two voices. Could it be our parents? My heart leaped into my throat forcing me to gasp! Shawna gave me a dirty look at the corner

of her eye that meant be quiet dummy you're going to get caught. It was only Maxine and Logan walking by. The two infirmary nobles. The villains that gave us brainwashing shots and "vitamins". I used to think they were pretty cool until I learned of their evil intent.

"How long do you think this crack has been here?" asked Maxine.

Her face was no longer one that seemed concerned. She was always so nice about you know, my needle hatred. Now her once gentle blue eyes seemed evil. Her puffy white hair with crooked glasses made me see in her an evil professor working for her cruel and unrelenting dictator of a boss. This new vision gave me chills. I think I might have some nightmares about people with white hair in lab coats. I tried to shake off these thoughts as Logan spoke.

"I'm not sure, no one is saying, everyone is so hush-hush about it," said, Logan.

He seemed genuinely lost. I am not sure how much Logan believes in VI-Counts methods. He doesn't seem to be as eager as Maxine to carry them out. His dirty blonde hair was always so neatly arranged, unlike Maxine's hair which was more like Shawna's in temperament. He was short but slim which seemed to make him look taller than he really was. He always seemed pleasantly cheerful. Which was in stark contrast to what he was displaying now. His green eyes looked torn.

"Elizabeth and Henry have a theory that it was a message delivery system used by the outsiders to pass notes from Tobey to Quinn," said Maxine.

Shawna looked over in my direction at the mention of Elizabeth and Henry. They were two of the other Nobles. They were twins, brother and sister. They looked similar but not identical. Elizabeth had ruby red hair with a bit of a fiery temperament which we were able to observe at our annual assemblies.

Here intense red hair made her emerald green eyes stand out even when standing by the back wall of the assembly. Henry on the other hand had blonde hair with honey brown eyes. He seemed a little more laid back in his delivery and posture. We really did not have any direct dealings with them. But Shawna and I were beginning to see that commutation doesn't seem to be so open between the master and his pawns. That made me even more fearful!

"It makes sense I am not sure how else the correspondence could've gotten into the Dome," said Logan.

"I still say what VI-Count did to Tobey was extreme! We could've given Toby the V–62 shot and completely wiped his memory banks. I mean we need all the bodies we can get for the expansion. It's gonna take a lot of room and provisions to make room for the Corp. in the Dome. That's 95 extra people! I'm still not sure why VI-Count is even bringing the Corp. in here. I mean isn't that the whole reason we're in the Dome in the first place, to be protected from the Corp. So why bring them in?" asked Maxine.

"Maxine, you know the V–62 isn't fully tested. That in itself could've killed Tobey. You need to be careful with what you say about VI-Count. You know he's added cameras and he has his Watchman working around the clock still. He is really shaken up by the intruders. We need to be careful what we are talking about. I do not want to have any dealings with that numbskull Danny, or the other goons, as for the Corp. I have no idea why he would make such a move. When the Lower class finds out there are going to be problems. Probably some rioting. But VI-Count assures us that he has them under control, whatever that means," said Logan cautiously with a bit of a tremble in his voice.

Seeing Logan this shaken up was making me even more nervous. I really did not like what we were hearing. I was starting to wonder if we should just leave before we learned anymore. I looked over at Shawna who clearly did not share my same concern. She was fully immersed and engrossed in Maxine and Logan's conversation.

"You're right! I am more worried about Hank. That guy turned his own mother in. How heartless can you be? I guess we better not talk out of line. Louis has already been called to the VI-Count twice this week." said Maxine regretfully.

Shawna looked over at me with the mention of Louis. She was the only Noble who didn't treat the Lower class like there are beneath them or lower slime. She would even stop to talk to the young ones in the corridors or even in the Center. Unlike the other Nobles who only came down at Assemblies. Even share jokes with us. She was on the taller side, and slim with red hair with green eyes, but not a cutting emerald green-like Elizabeth. Louis's eyes were more natural, and calming. They were closer to a sea green. Yet she could be feisty, turning her calm gentle eyes into more of a violent stormy sea when necessary. That was very rare and only with good reason.

"What? Why?" asked Logan in a shocked tone.

"Louis wasn't happy with VI-Count's decision concerning Tobey. Then when she learned about Quinn being held in the lower cell as a prisoner, she was outraged. She said he was only a kid. And that VI-Count is supposed to protect all who live in the Dome and he wasn't living up to his role as our leader," said Maxine.

This revelation about Louis gave Shawna and me a bit of hope. Maybe not everyone is so happy to be under VI-Counts controlling thumb so to speak.

"Wow! Not smart! She putting herself in danger talking out against VI-Count like that! Quinn isn't a kid! He's 17 and he's a danger to the Dome and all that we stand for. He's an outsider, a contaminant," spat Logan.

A danger to the Dome! If anyone is a danger to the Dome it is VI-Count and Lord Byron I thought to myself outraged!

"I know but he is still human. And he is Tobey's
son," said Maxine.

"What? He is Tobey's son! I had no idea. How is that even possible? All the children are here! There shouldn't be any children on the outside. Quinn had to be around five years old when the rebels were persuaded to turn over their children. Tobey must've hidden Quinn somewhere and came into the Dome on his own. But why? Why would he leave his son?" Questioned Logan confusion filling his features.

He ran his hand through his dirty blonde hair trying to take in the gravity of what Maxine had just said. I was with him, my mind whirling as well.

"You know what VI-Count did as well as I do. He did not leave any parent a choice. They had to give up their children if they wanted their children to live and if they wanted to keep their own lives. So Tobey must have never registered Quinn. That's probably why VI-Count has seemed a bit edgier. Which makes sense because if

Quinn was hidden and is alive after all these years, there may be others." said Maxine gravely.

"Man, no wonder VI-Count has been more unusual. He must be worried about a possible mutiny forming," said Logan understanding sinking in.

"How is Quinn responding to V-61?" Asked Maxine.

"Somehow it's not having an effect on him. I am not sure why. We have tried it on another lower class named Lizzy. She told us everything we asked without a problem. Quinn seems to have a resistance to V-61," said Logan baffled.

"That is strange. Did you get any unusual information from Lizzy?" questioned Maxine.

"No, not really. She didn't know anything about the rebel intruders. She was innocent." said Logan disappointed.

"Do you know whom I think we should get a hold of?" added Maxine.

"Lucas! I know he's involved somehow," fumed Logan.

"Maybe we should bring our suspicions to VI-Count and try V-61 on Lucas." suggested Maxine.

"Why that would be a great idea, Maxine," said Lord Byron.

"Good evening, Lord Byron," said Maxine with a tremble in her voice.

"Evening Sir," said Logan timidly.

"So, you're both conspiring on what would be best, are you? Have ideas for VI-Count do you?" question Lord Byron with displeasure.

"Not really sure, we were merely talking," said Logan shakily.

"You know talking can lead to bigger things. Like action against our leader. The leader of the Dome," said Lord Byron.

"No sir! Nothing like that at all!" said Maxine fearfully.

"Glad to hear. How was the testing coming along on Quinn?" asked Lord Byron.

"We are still tweaking the formula. To be honest, he hasn't responded yet sir," said Logan.

"Keep working on it. We need answers. Like where did he come from? We have five children here and there should not be any more. VI-Count made sure of that," said Lord Byron darkly.

At the sound of menace in his voice, all the hairs stood up on the back of my neck and my blood ran cold.

"Yes sir, we are headed to the infirmary now," said Logan desperate to get away from Lord Byron.

The three went on their way without another word. Shawna looked over at me with pure dread in her eyes. My heart has come down out of my throat but now it rests on the tunnel floor. What did Lord Byron mean by VI-court making sure of that? It could only mean one thing. It was horrible to say out loud, horrible to think. Only five children remain. That's me, Shawna, Tyler, Maddy, and Dimitri.
We are the five. So our parents didn't have a choice. They had to turn us over to VI-Count to protect us. Or the Corp. would kill us and them. Quinn's father is no longer around thanks to VI-Count, the very man who is supposed to be our protector. Poor Quinn that has to be so hard. To lose a father. To not be able to be with him. Why was Toby in the Dome and not on the outside? Who raised Quinn? Because a five-year-old could not raise himself. This I knew for sure.

The fact that the Dome has a prisoner and that the prisoner is a child gives me goosebumps! One that they are trying to give some sort of truth serum to. Gives me chills. They want to find out about this mysterious person, his life, and the outsiders.

The Dome keeps sinking lower and lower in my safety meter. VI-Count must feel very threatened. The hidden cameras, 24-hour Watchman. What did Logan mean by VI-Count acting more unusual? And what's with all the V somethings? Logan and Maxine have been experimenting on us! I felt so gross inside, playing guinea pig and not even knowing it! Why would VI-Count move the Corp. into the Dome? The very one who destroyed innocent families and children? Isn't he supposed to protect us from the Corp? My head was spinning from all the new information.

Chapter 13

"We need to warn Lucas. He's in danger and doesn't even know it," whispered Shawna.

"We will. Let's put the clothes in the drop location, then we'll find Lucas." I said reassuringly.

Carefully we looked around making sure no one was in sight. Then we pushed the bag as far back under the overhang as possible so it would not be seen by anyone who was passing by. We worked our way back to the center without using the tunnel of destain. I had had enough of that tunnel for a lifetime. As we headed back we had to pass by the infirmary where Maxine and Logan were cleaning up for the evening. Maxine locked eyes with me and called out. I felt a chill.

"Hello, Sebastian and Shawna. What are you two up to?"

"Hello," I said as cautiously as possible trying not to let my voice betray me.

I felt like they were looking into my brain reading my thoughts, knowing that Shawna and I had overheard their conversation. Seeing that we knew the truth about the shots and the "vitamins". I must have been holding my breath and my muscles a little too tightly because Logan spoke up and asked

"Sebastian, are you OK? You don't look so good."

"I'm fine," I said trying to shake off their penetrating eyes.

I have to get out of here. I felt trapped claustrophobic even. One million times worse than that stupid old tunnel. I would welcome the tunnel at this point. Please, get me out of here I wanted to scream at Shawna! I feel like Shawna was reading my mind and she abruptly jumped in and said

"We were on our way to the center for some ping-pong."

"Oh, OK well have fun. We will see both of you next week," said Maxine cheerfully.

"Next week, for what?" I asked startled.

"For your, six-month shot and exam," said Logan slowly.

"Oh right, see you then," I said nervously.

"Are you sure you're OK Sebastian? Maybe you should sit down for a minute. You're acting a bit funny," said Maxine concerned.

If I didn't just over here that conversation I would've thought, used to think even that she was genuinely concerned.

"He's fine, he always gets a little weird about ping-pong. A little too much pressure to win I guess," reassured Shawna.

After that lame excuse, which I did not think anyone in their right mind would ever believe, we left rather quickly. Under the pretense of an epic ping-pong game. I really hoped Lucas and Dimitri was there. Most nights they were. But it could be that this night since we needed them to be there, they would be off welding somewhere. I looked over at Shawna and she seemed a bit frustrated. I asked what was wrong. That was a huge mistake.

"You numbskull! What are you trying to do to get us caught? Your face and body language screamed guilt! You have got to get yourself under control! We have to get to Lucas and warn him. Which we will not be able to do if you can't pull yourself together." Shawna lectured.

She continued on in that fashion for longer than I would have liked to be berated. No offense to Shawna but I tuned her out. Something else had grabbed my attention completely. I saw in the Center Lucas and Dimitri. I let out a loud sigh and shouted, "There!"

"Shouting is not gonna help!" Shawna growled quietly, then together we walked over to Lucas and Dimitri.

"Hey, guys!" Dimitri called out happily.

"Hey, can we play?" Shawna said.

"Of course. I've beaten Lucas for the hundredth time this evening I could use a new challenge. That is if you're any good." Dimitri jeered.

"Bring it!" Shawna exclaimed.

But not before telling me to take a seat beside Lucas and reminding me that I have to calmly tell him what we heard. This seemed like one of the toughest things I've ever had to do. She was asking me to do the impossible. How do you calmly go up to someone and say 'Hey someone wants to give you an injection with a needle so they can use all the information in your brain to rat others out to a evil dictator who is bent on who knows what really'. I know better than to present this question to Shawna, so I simply went with the opposite of what I was feeling.

"Got it!" I said not wanting to let her down.

Shawna was really good but so was Dimitri. It was a fun game to watch. It was a bit distracting at first. Shawna then cut me a look which meant hurry up. So I averted my eyes from the match and focused on Lucas.

"Lucas we overheard Logan and Maxine today," I said.

"Well?" Lucas said impatiently.

"Maxine told Logan it was you that she wanted to get a hold of because she thinks you were involved somehow. Logan is convinced you are involved too! Maxine suggested taking the matter to VI-Count. They want to give you a shot called V-61." I said gravely.

"V-61, that's the truth serum! I can put our whole mission in jeopardy and endanger many lives. They can't do that!" spat Lucas.

"That's not all. Lord Byron, he's very suspicious, and he even accused Maxine and Logan of conspiring against VI-Count." I said.

"I knew that VI-Count was getting paranoid and I guess he should be," said Lucas.

"Lord Byron said there should be only five children. And that Quinn shouldn't even exist. What do they mean by the Corp. took care of that? And why is Quinn not responding to V-61?" I questioned unsure if I even wanted to know the answer.

"There's a lot that I don't think you're ready to hear Sebastian," said Lucas cautiously.

"Try me!" I said eager to have someone provide some type of clarity.

"Let me answer one question at a time. VI-Count thanks there are only five children because that's the number the Corp gave them. All they knew to exist. The Corp was to silence the rebellion. What better way to get people to stop than taking away what meant the most of them," Lucas sadly.

"There children," I said with realization.

"Sebastian, please know that your father and mother love you very much. They had to turn you over to VI-Count. It was the only way. The Corp is greedy and they would remove any obstacle in their way, using any means necessary! VI-Count promised your parents that he would keep your children safe. That you all would not have to spend your life running from the Corp. It was the hardest decision your parents had to make. I am sure it was equally as hard for them now to get you involved in this dangerous assignment. But they trust you and believe in you," said Lucas.

looking at me with deep pride in his eyes, something which I had never seen from him while talking to me.

"They told you that?" I said moved.

"Yes, they did. And much more. As for Quinn well, there are others like Quinn. Others had children but never registered them. It was like they didn't exist. They hid their children from the VI-Count and from the Corp. Many families did not join the rebellion. They were afraid for the safety of their children and for themselves. They sent their children to live with someone else, one who would raise them, free from the Corp. and from VI-Count. These families lived out of the bounds of Corp control. It was an ultimate sacrifice for both mother and father. If the Corp. got a hold of anyone, they would be worked like slaves making steel, concrete, and other goods. The Corp. worked them to death on building projects. All to fuel the Crops. take over. So,

Tobey, that's Quinn's father, handed over Quinn to one of these families to protect and care for him until he was old enough for them to reunion together again," said Lucas.

I cut Lucas off and asked, "Wait, what about Quinn's mom?"

"The Corp. got a hold of her and sadly she didn't make it. She would not give up Tobey or Quinn's location. An example was set by the Corp. All could see what would happen if you were caught, so you see Sebastian getting caught is not an option. That's another reason why your parents have waited until now. They needed to wait until you were old enough to see VI-Count for who he really was. And to be able to help with the uprising from the inside," said Lucas.

"But what are you doing here? And how do you know so much?" I asked impatiently.

"I was a rebel along with your parents Shawna's parents and the others. I came in undercover along with Tobey. Our assignment was to get into the Dome, protect and watch over the five children who were taken," said Lucas.

"Tobey gave up being able to be a father to his son and you gave up your freedom just to look after us," I said.

"Yes, but Tobey and Quinn have been able to work together for the last 3 years. And Quinn understood the decision his father made and he wasn't resentful," said Lucas.

"How did Tobey get caught?" I asked.

"Tobey's disloyalty to VI-Count was discovered one night by the Watchman. A Watchman named Brutus. He is not someone to mess with! He was hidden and was able to see Tobey and Quinn's exchange." Said Lucas.

"An exchange of what? What could be so serious for VI-Count to take someone's life?" I asked.

"Brutus saw Tobey receive a letter from Quinn. They were using a message delivery system," Logan said.

"You mean the crack in the Dome wall in the west wing?" I cut them off to ask.

"Yes, aka the crack. Brutus did not turn in Tobey right away. He waited two weeks, he was trying to see if anyone else was involved. When Brutus felt like it would be too risky to withhold information any longer from VI-Count. He turned him in. When Tobey was turned over to VI-Count he made an example out of him for all who might be thinking about rebelling. No one has seen or heard from Tobey since then. The message was clear. VI-Count like the Corp. will not tolerate disloyalty," Lucas said gravely.

"Does Quinn know?" I asked saddened by the thought.

"Yes, he got word. He knew he had been spotted so he did the best he could to hide. But one of the Watchman, one named Aaron found Quinn. But before he was found he was able to dose up on the needed medicine to counteract the V-61," said Lucas.

"That's why Maxine said it wasn't working," I said understanding dawned on me.

"You got it. But it won't last forever. The medicine will wear off soon. That's why we have to get him out and quickly," said Lucas urgently.

"Why an uprising? Why now? My parents had said in the note that VI-Count has lied, what do they mean?" I rapid-fired questions at Lucas craving understanding more and more by the moment.

"They're right, VI-Count has lied. You see our plan all along was to get your children back to your parents somehow. We thought that VI-Count was going to help. He told us all that if the parents handed their children over, he would protect them and when the Corp. wasn't so focused on capturing the rebels and their families, then all could come and join in living in the Dome. Remaining under VI-Count's protection. But when the parents confronted VI-Count he told them that they would never see their children again. And if they tried he would relocate the children so they can never be found. They saw VI-Count for the first time, who he really was. He had lied to them from the beginning and taken what they valued most. But they refused to be defeated. So they started planning what is now called the Uprising, to free not only five children but also all other Lower-class members. The Dome is a prison. No one can ever leave. No Lower-class member will ever become a Noble. It's all been a lie. No one will ever be able to have a different plan or idea from VI-Count while under his control. He holds all power. He is hungry like a ravenous wolf and fights to keep control and power no matter whom he has to take down. But we know it's our time, our time to rise and take him out of power. So we can regain our freedom and our families. Something that we have all longed for these last 12 years. We have to stop VI-Count and his lies," said Lucas with a fierce determination on his face turning his light complexion red.

"Tyler, Dimitri, and Maddy's parents are they still alive," I asked not sure if I wanted to know the answer.

"Sadly no Sebastian. They too were taken by the Corp. and all worked until they could not work any longer," Lucas explained gravely.

"What will they do, ya know, without parents?" I asked.

"We cannot think that far ahead at this moment Sebastian. We need to keep our minds clear, sharp, and focused. So that we are not caught off guard. The Watchman is on high alert, and the Wolf is ready to fight to the death to defend his territory. We can not have answers to all our questions right now. Be patient, keep focused," said Lucas while keeping eye contact.

His patient blue eyes speak to me just as loud as his words. He seemed to make sure that I was hearing every word he said. I sat quietly next to Lucas allowing this new information to sink in. I had learned so much so fast it was hard to keep all the facts straight. I had to know the truth about their parents, so I tried again to find the answer.

"Do they know about their parents?" I whispered.

"No" was all Lucas whispered, barely audible.

Chapter 14

I knew not to try to push Lucas any further. I could tell our conversation was over. He was exhausted. This could not be easy for Lucas, he had been carrying this reality and weight for years as I have only just learned a fragment of truth. Shawna and Dimitri finished up their game. I too was exhausted. Both Shawna and Dimitri played ten rounds of ping pong. They had been playing nonstop for the last hour. They were clearly equally matched.

Tyler had left over an hour ago claiming to be bored before the match even started. But he had been watching Lucas and Dimitri play for about half an hour before we arrived. Maddy was in the chair off to my left. I didn't notice it and I wasn't sure how long, but she was watching me. I wasn't sure what was going through her mind. Her brown eyes deeply examined me. I felt like she was trying to hear and understand what Lucas was saying to me. She seemed almost jealous not to be part of the conversation. My mind and heart were full of deep sorrow for her and for the others. It didn't seem fair that we got to have our parents and they didn't. My stomach sank as I thought about sharing the notes from our parents with them. I'm sure it made them think about the possibility that their parents were out there somewhere. That they two might receive a note in the near future. I hated this! I hated the Dome! I hated the Corp! I hated VI-Count! I hated not knowing! I hated the uncertainty of it all! Everything was falling apart around me. I felt like I was shattering along with it, unable to piece myself back together. I didn't know what was worse, to live in a twisted fake illusion of safety and protection feeling like everything is normal, or finding out that your entire life has been a lie and constructed by an evil cruel puppet master. One who is so manipulative he would stop at nothing, nothing to get what he wants.

All of this was crushing me. I was overwhelmed with fatigue and a sudden strong urge to sleep. Maddy who was watching me called Shawna over in alarm. Shawna noticed that I was starting to lean over to the side. She knew I was about to fall asleep from sheer exhaustion. She knew she had to get me back to my room before I fell over adding another wound to my ever-growing list.

Without me being able to walk on my own they would never be able to return me to my room. Someone might call Logan or Maxine and take me to the infirmary. We definitely didn't want that to happen!

"Sebastian don't you even think about it. Don't you fall asleep!" Begged Shawna.

"We need to get him to his room! He really doesn't look good. We need to get him out of here before Logan and Maxine come by," said Maddy worried.

"He's had a bit of a rough day, to say the least. It's all caught up with him," said Shawna trying to use my odd behavior.

With the help of Dimitri, Maddy, and Shawna I made it back to my quarters. I did not even remember getting into bed. Not even the sleep-stealing sheets could rob me of sleep that night. It was the first night I actually slept in my bed in years. Dimitri and Maddy didn't know that I slept on the floor. Shawna knew but she must not mentioned it. I faintly remembered Maddy asking if I was going to be all right. But before I could reply, I was out to the world.

Chapter 15

That night my dreams were so realistic upon waking it took me some time to figure out what was reality and what wasn't. Ironically, that in itself was my reality. In my dream, Lucas was given the V-61 and VI-Count learned about the Uprising. Shawna's parents and my parents were given V-62 and it did just as expected. It completely erased their memory. When I was finally allowed to see them they just stared at me blankly. I whispered Mom, Dad. They told me that I must be mistaken because they never had kids. They didn't even remember that they were married! Their expression looked confused. A deep sadness covered their face reinforced by their slumped shoulders. They look so defeated. I woke in a cold sweat suddenly.

Determined not to let VI-Count get his hands on Lucas or my parents. I sat up and surveyed my surroundings. I got up and had a quick muffin for some kind of nourishment. Again with no time to chew or enjoy its flavor. Not that there was even anything to enjoy about it. I had to get back to

Shawna. But then a thought occurred to me that it would be obvious to anyone who may be watching.

Lord Byron already saw me going in the opposite direction of my work assignment earlier. I can't raise any more suspicion. I need to go to my work assignment first. I need to be as normal as possible. This was not going to be easy! I grabbed my tool bag and headed out the door. My mind spun to what to do and what would be the best way to get to Shawna. As I was headed to the East wing I slowed as I went past the Greenhouse. Tyler was going up and down the road gathering our main staple potatoes. He was so irritating.

He always seemed to show off with everything he did. Even the way he hurried up and down the rows pacing everyone else. His morning collection is already overflowing out of his bushel baskets. It was taking a toll on him through. His face was red from exertion and his dark hair was even darker as he was soaked with perspiration. I tried to let my irritation at Tyler go. Lucas told me last night among many other things that Tyler didn't feel good enough.

That was why he always tried to overcompensate with everything. He just didn't want anyone to figure out how broken he felt inside, or how lost he was. I tried to view Tyler through these new lenses but it was still so difficult. But I had to give him props. He was holding himself together no matter how fragmented it really was.

I saw that I had made the correct decision. Everyone is playing it cool. This was new to me I reassured myself. Tyler, Dimitri, and Maddy have been at this longer than me and Shawna. They've had more time to process and adjust to the idea that their lives have been, you know a lie. Tyler must've noticed me watching because he gave me a What are you doing you idiot look. Good old Tyler.

When I made it to the East wing expansion site there was the crane operator, she was waiting for me. More proof that I had made the correct choice. The expansion looked different to me now. No longer was I filled with excitement at the prospect of eating something other than potatoes. Instead, that excitement was replaced with concern. It still looked the same with the

steel beams in neat stacks, and concrete bags next to
their mixers for the smaller jobs.

A few piles of dirt that had been shifted to clear the way for the beams to be put in position. The glass panels over on the far wall glinted in the morning's first rays. All looked the same physically, but inside it took on a darker light. Darkness unable to be undone by the sunlight. The crane and its imposing silhouette ready to carry VI-Counts dirty work was a glaring reminder of the truth. I had a shiver run down my spine at the reality of it all. How was I gonna do this? I was up against a lunatic, a madman. I was no match for VI-Count. I heard my name called out which brought me out of my thoughts. Our crane operator Kelly was trying to get my attention. She was nice but she was kind of running out of patience since over the last few weeks she hasn't been able to do her job at all. She was short with a dark complexion like Shawna.

But her hair didn't seem to have the same kind of mind of his own as Shawna's. It was short with tight jet-black curls. She was in her late 30s. 38 to be exact. I only knew this because I overheard a conversation between her and Aki. I think he likes her. He was trying to give her a compliment but I don't think it worked out too well. He told her that she was muscular for a woman.

She retorted back that he had less hair than most men she knew. I could see Aki's cheeks turn red with embarrassment even through his caramel complexion. He quickly backtracked but Kelly had a good sense of humor. She just started laughing at the face he made and told him thanks, I think. Aki smiled sheepishly back saying ditto. They continued on in their conversation. I learned that he was only a year older than Kelly.

She could be a bit intimidating if you didn't know her. I knew her well, but I still approached slowly due to her growing impatience. Not with me but with the situation.

"Good morning Kelly," I said.

"Good! What's good about it? My crane still isn't up and running. I am a crane operator without a crane! So Sebastian let me ask you, what could possibly be good about this morning? Kelly ranted. Her usual calm ocean-like blue eyes were in turmoil. She was in a mood and I knew that I better tread very lightly.

"Right, I have my tools right here. I will get right to it," I said shyly.

Hoping not to be on the receiving end of her frustration.

"Look, Sebastian. I'm sorry I snapped. I'm not mad at you. I'm just frustrated. I don't understand what keeps happening. You've always figured out what is up with the equipment and quickly. It's never taken you this long. And Lord Byron has been breathing down my neck every day. I just can't stand that guy, he gives me the creeps," explained Kelly still fuming.

The red on her cheeks penetrated even through her dark complexion. As I was trying to listen to Kelly I was looking around for possible cameras. The ceilings were so high I didn't see how any camera would even be able to have a clear enough image from that distance. She noticed me not paying attention to her conversation anymore so she interrupted my thoughts.

"I can catch a hint I'll let you get back to work," she said coldly.

Oh no I have added insult to injury here! I braced myself and explained.

"No, no, it's not like that. I was just looking around for cameras," I blurted out loud without fully thinking it out.

"Cameras, why would there be cameras? This is a construction site Sebastian, not a stage, " she said firmly.

"Right, good point. Dumb me, what was I thinking?" I said trying to backtrack.

But Kelly wasn't stupid. I kicked myself. If Shawna knew what I just did she be kicking me too.

"Sebastian, are you OK? You look perplexed. Is there something wrong? You know that you can talk to me, right?" She asked genuinely concerned.

Her expression softened to the Kelly that I know. Her stormy eyes were now calm and gentle. No, no I can not look at her eyes! I will end up spilling the beans and then where would I be? I steeled myself ready to not give away any more information.

"I know I can, but it's complicated. Don't worry I'm fine. Let me get to work so we can get this thing back online for you." I said.

"Ok," she said unconvinced.

She eyed me seriously as I walked over to the crane. For some reason, I had to focus extra hard not to trip on the uneven ground. I had never noticed how uneven it was until now. It seemed as if it was growing more and more uneven by the minute. Reaching out with a mind of its own trying to grab at my feet. Boy, I am going to go crazy if this goes on too long! Snap out of it Sebastian I yelled at myself inside so as to not draw any more attention from Kelly.

I knew what the problem with the crane was already. I knew how to fix it. But I couldn't let Kelly knows that. My mission was to keep the crane from running. And Kelly wasn't a dummy. She knew a bit about the machine she operated. It wouldn't be long before Kelly would check the fuses for herself. The only reason she hasn't so far is that she probably thinks that I have already checked them. I was starting to get nervous. Not sure how long I could stop the crane's operation. Now with Kelly standing right there next to me watching I knew I was not going to be able to stall much longer.

A part of me was so frustrated I really didn't like the idea of Kelly thinking I couldn't figure it out. I always could figure things out and she knew that. And I also wondered if Kelly knew what she was doing whom she was helping. I mean this expansion was so that VI-Count could bring in the Corp. I knew Kelly and I knew she would not be eager to do her job if she had all the facts. I didn't know any Lower-class members who would participate in bringing the Corp. into the Dome. The very ones we needed protection from. What would bringing in the Corp. do to the Dome. Ninety-five people who didn't care about the environment, people, or their lives. People were expendable to them, mere objects used to get a job done. If that isn't the definition of greed I don't know what is. What dangers would we face with them on the inside? We all function well in the Dome. The lower class anyway. And Louis, one of the Nobles was actually pretty cool. She's the only one that ever talked to Lower-class members like we were humans instead of lower lifeforms.

Louis was funny even telling me a joke
every now and then. Though she could be quite
fiery as well. Must be the red hair part of her is
what Lucas always liked to say. Not sure what the
color of someone's hair has to do with anything. I
mean Shawna's hair is black and so is your mom
but they're both feisty as they come. I was yanked
back into the moment by a distinct and menacing
voice.

"Progress report Kelly," VI-Count demanded
more than asked.

"No action sir," Kelly replied.

"And why not? It's been three weeks. We
cannot afford to lose any more time. Cold
weather is coming. We must have the Dome
expansion complete before the storms begin,"
demanded VI-Count.

That's his fabrication I thought to myself.
What a liar! It took all I had not to scream in his
face, telling him what a monster he really was.
But I kept it together I knew that would only make
matters worse. I was literally biting my tongue a
little too hard I realized because there was a hint
of
blood.

"Yes sir, but I can not complete my task without a working crane sir," said Kelly as calmly as possible in her frustrated, irritated state. I was very impressed by her ability to keep it together despite VI-Counts cold tone.

"Why hasn't it been fixed by now!" demanded VI-Count.

"The boy here is supposed to be working on it. But maybe he is the problem and not the solution," said Lord Byron with hate dripping from his accusation against me.

This made my face flush with heat and rage, it was increasingly difficult to keep collected. What does he mean by the boy?

"The boy is not a problem sir. I guarantee it. Sebastian is our best mechanic. He will figure it out," Kelly said with pride and confidence in her voice.

Her defense made me want to crawl into a hole and hide my face. Here Kelly is defending me when I should not be defended. Now torn between rage and embarrassment, I was losing what was up. I was feeling a bit overwhelmed and needed this engagement to end soon or I might just lose it permanently. If only Kelly knew that I was the one who had a solution but was not fixing it. I felt like I should tell her. I felt like I owed it to her.

Maybe with her being in the know, we could have a greater chance of a crane malfunction. I mean if she could maybe accidentally damage something that would take a couple of weeks to repair. Or better yet something that couldn't be replaced. I knew it was risky. But I felt like it was more of a risk not telling her. She's not stupid and she's going to figure out that I have a solution for the crane yet have chosen not to fix it. That would not go over well.

What would I say then? It might be too late. Besides it wouldn't be long before they would bring in Lizzy. She was the other mechanic in the Dome. She was good but not great. She was still being trained. So it may take her a while to figure out the problem but not long. She would know to check the fuses before going too deep into the machine. Telling Kelly the truth was probably our only hope of keeping the crane down and disabled for any period of time.

"Boy," VI-Count called out.

"Me sir?" I asked dumbly even though I knew that he was talking to me. I tried to keep the venom out of my voice.

"You have until the end of the day. If it isn't fixed by then you'll be fired. No longer used as a mechanic here in the Dome. We will have another job for you boy," Vl-Count said coldly, sending shivers up and down my spine with the thought of what he could mean by another job...

"That's not fair," I started to protest but Kelly cut me off.

"He'll have it done!" she said firmly.

"He better," said Vl-Count coldly.

Then Lord Byron and Vl-Count left the work site.

Kelly turned her ocean-like blue eyes to me and gently said "Sebastian, you need to tell me what is going on. Vl-Count doesn't just come down to the lower floors of the Dome. Something is up and I need to know. I want to be able to help and protect you."

That was it, I had to tell her, I didn't have a choice. I braced myself. I mean it isn't the easier story to believe. I still don't know if I believe it all myself.

Chapter 16

"You have to promise not to tell anyone. This can put not just me but a lot of people in danger," I said feeling all noted up inside.

"I promise as long as it will not put you in any danger by not speaking up," she said calmly.

"OK, it's a long story. The condensed version is we need to the crane in disrepair," I said matter of factly.

"Why would we need to do that? And who is we?" Kelly demanded cutting me off.

"Let me finish. It will make sense when I'm done. Hopefully," I said.

"Ok," she said unsure.

"VI-Count is eager and on edge because there have been ones who have infiltrated the Dome. They are the ones who are sabotaging the crane. Well, at least it was first. Then I found a note," I said.

"A note, from who?" Kelly asked me more curious than annoyed.

"My parents," I barely squeaked out trying to hold back tears from saying my parents out loud.

"You mean Stella and Emmett?" Kelly asked.

"You know my parents," I asked shocked.

"Yes, Stella is my sister," Kelly exclaimed.

"Your sister. How could that be?" I said.

I mean it does make sense, maybe. They have similar complexions. They both have beautiful ocean-like blue eyes. And there was always a connection that Kelly and I shared, a similarity that she had I felt from someone that was in my past. But I can never put my finger on it, until now. Kelly always did stand up for me and told me she was proud of me. She checked on me from time to time. But now I guess it's because here I am her nephew. She was nice to the others but not to the degree that she had always been to me.

"Why are you here in the Dome while my mom is on the outside, and why didn't you ever tell me that you were my aunt?" I asked.

"Sebastian, it's a long and sad story. Let's just say your mom and I didn't see eye to eye. I thought coming to the Dome would be a better life, a safer life than the one outside of the Dome. I never told you that I was your aunt because I thought it might be too painful for you and I also knew you would ask questions. Questions that I didn't want to have to answer. Sorry if that sounds self, I guess it is, but I just wanted to move forward from that life, the one before the Dome. I never joined the rebellion, like all the others here. Well, almost all. Stella, your mom that is was so set on fighting the Corp. She said no one would have a future if we didn't stand up, but the earth was so damaged by then. No one could deny global warming. The weather was getting more and more erratic. The air was so full of smog we needed respirators most days just to be able to breathe outside safely. There was no safe water to be found. The Corp and other corporations like it had completely taken away any chance of living on the outside. There was no life to be had outside the Dome. Your parents had to choose. They now live underground. I didn't want that. And I couldn't forgive her for giving you up Sebastian. I do love her and miss her. I am so glad to hear that she's alive. She and Emmett, your father. You know that's where you got your gift from. The one you have with mechanics. That came from your father," Kelly said with tears in her eyes. Her eyes looked more than sad from what was going now in the present. In her eyes, I could see so much sadness, so much grief, and loss. Her shoulders looked so weighted down as if the weight of all humankind was placed squarely on her shoulders alone. This was too much for one person. I suddenly felt guilty for bringing up so much pain for Kelly. It hurt me deeply to see her so distressed.

"I know," was all I could muster.

"Sorry. I interrupted you again. Where were you? Let's get back to what you were saying," said Kelly, trying to regain her composure.

I had to tell her, didn't I? I mean I kind of already started. There was no way for me to turn back now.

"VI-Count is expanding the Dome to bring in the Corp. Ninety-five people that are responsible for the condition of the earth as well as the cruelty to people," I said.

"What? But why would he want to do such a thing? It doesn't make any sense," Kelly asked baffled and enraged.

"He is, you have to believe me. He is not the man he says he is." I said pleading my voice cracking.

"I believe you, Sebastian" replied Kelly.

I was so relieved to hear Kelly say that I collapsed into her arms and balled like a baby. I had to. I had to let some of the pressure off. It was too much. I needed someone who cared about me. Someone I could trust.

"So what are we gonna do about it? We have to get the crane up and running somehow. VI-Count is definitely watching us. We need to get it up and running so that nothing happens to you. I definitely don't trust Lord Byron and now I have learned that I can not trust VI-Count. He might hurt you, and we can't have that. I would never be able to forgive myself." said Kelly mournfully.

"I was hoping that maybe you could ya know, break something kind of important to the crane's ability to run," I said sheepishly.

"Now you want me to get fired!" Said Kelly as she laughed and tasseled my hair.

Kelly had always done that. I liked it when I was little but I thought I was getting a bit too old for it now. We had more pressing issues to work on than me bringing out about how I was too old for her to be messing up my hair though. We had a crane to fix, and then break again quickly. It felt good. To talk to Kelly. I was still nervous though because she did trust VI-Count before and never joined the rebellion. She blamed my mom for leaving me. It must've been hard for her and my mom to go through so much and then to be separated for so long.

Chapter 17

It only took five minutes to fix the crane. I put a fresh fuse in then, bolted the metal panels back in place. I felt a tinge of guilt because my parents told me to keep the crane in disrepair for as long as possible. Instead, I fixed it. VI-Counts evil plans would be able to move forward. I was beating myself up when I noticed the stack of steel beams 20 feet high, and 100 feet long. Alongside endless pallets of concrete the quickset kind.

Time is of the essence when you have such massive beams to secure. It had to be done quickly. The Corp. who worked people into the ground. Forcing them to work in their factories and plants taking raw material in to forge steel. To mix sand, stone, and lime to make concrete. While others were forced to work unceasingly on building projects.

Why would VI-Count want to bring in the Corp? The ones behind such cruelty. VI-Count must have needed their supplies to expand the infrastructure of the Dome. Was that the Corps?

terms? That if they provided the supplies, then they could live in the Dome? I mean where else could VI-Count get the supplies?

Now that I think about it, where did he get the supplies? Are they needed to build the Dome in

the first place? Wasn't the Corp. the only one who had a monopoly on steel and concrete? What about the other supplies? Where did they come from? I knew that our clothing was made here in the Dome, but where did the fabric come for the clothing? Or lumber for the furniture? Where did the ping-pong table come from? And why ping-pong?

I was getting more and more lost in questions as I observed my surroundings. Lightbulbs, flooring, shoes, the crane, where did it all come from? Where did we even get the crane now that I think of it? So much was just considered normal. No one seemed to stop or question let alone think about how it was that we actually had all we needed. I was beginning to see the cost of living in the Dome. Living life passively had taken its toll. Something I knew I would never be able to do again. How could this be happening not just to me, but to all the Lower-class members with the exception of a few. Could it be the vitamins that played a part in our oblivious existence? Would it be better not to exist at all than to live a lie? I'm not sure how much time is past, but when I finally blinked my eyes a few times to try to bring myself back to the present I noticed that Kelly was looking at me with concern.

I knew that I had given her an unexpected burden, but I really didn't feel that it could've been helped. I felt like she was telling me with her eyes to be calm, and that we would get through
this together. I so hoped that that would be true. I was returning her gaze with what I hoped to be a reassuring and confident expression. I wanted her to know that I trusted her, which was true. Now when I looked in those eyes the eyes so similar to my mother's I felt peace and comfort. I felt closer to my mother knowing that I had Kelly here with me. I knew she would protect me to the best of her ability. Lucas walked in interrupting our silent conversation. Unlike Kelly's ocean-like blue eyes, Lucas's blue eyes were

piercing. Not in a scary way but in a way that I felt as
though he could see that I had slipped up and told someone about the plan. I was anxious to know how he would react if he knew.
His light brown hair looked darker due to perspiration. He must have had a tough job already this morning. His gray long-sleeve shirt and red vest were riddled with burn holes from welding. Even his boots had burn marks. His face looked tired. It looked like he hadn't gotten much sleep the night before. I couldn't blame him. I don't think I could've slept either with Maxine and Logan out to get me with her brain-wiping serum. As Lucas approached he seemed to regain a bit of energy pulling his shoulders back when he spotted Kelly.

"Lucas!" Kelly greeted him warmly.

"Kelly, so nice to see you," said Lucas with a bit of extra color on his cheeks. Matching the color of his vest, deep red.

"What brings you down to the expansion site? And why not Dimitri?" Kelly questioned with a little red appearing on her cheeks as well.

However, not as evidenced as Lucas since she has a darker complexion than him. Her eyes seemed to sparkle a little when she looked at Lucas. If I didn't know better you would think that they both like each other. Not like her in Aki, he was the only one that did the liking.

"Dimitri is finishing up on his own at the previously damaged site in the West wing. He's able to clean up on his own. He's actually come quite a long way. I am very proud of him. He is a great welder my only complaint is that he has to start using his welder's glove to cover the welded seam when he's chipping the slag way. A stray piece went down the back of my shirt today and burnt me about five times before I could get a hold of it to keep it away from my skin long enough for it to cool down so that I could get it out." Lucas said with a slight chuckle at the memory.

"Ouch! That sounds painful! But I am sure it was maybe a little entertaining to see you hopping around," said Kelly with a snicker.

"Dimitri did get a good laugh out of it. He said if gorillas could dance, that's what I would look like. But one quick cold glance for me cut that story short," Lucas explained happily.

I have never heard Lucas talk about Dimitri before. But you could hear and see the depth of his affection for Dimitri. It almost seemed that Lucas had a fatherly affection for Dimitri. I felt a bit of relief. I mean his parents are gone, but he would have Lucas to care for him. He had someone. But what about Tyler and Maddy? I still wasn't feeling so good about them not having anyone. I even felt sorry for Tyler even though he was, well you know, Tyler.

"What brings you down here?" I repeated Kelly's question since Lucas didn't seem to hear it the first time because I was equally as curious.

"Right, I came down to talk to you, Sebastian. I wanted to see how it was going with the repair work on the crane. I know you have been having a hard time getting it fixed. I wanted to come to see if I could give you a hand," said Lucas I found it very odd.

I didn't believe his excuse at all. What could be his real motive for coming all the way down to the East Wing?

"That is so sweet of you Lucas. No need to fear though, Sebastian here has a gift. He knows his machines and how to fix them. Why did he just finish repairing the crane before you came? It was just a silly old fuse that kept the crane down for three weeks. Who knew a fuse could keep an experienced mechanic from fixing the crane for so long," Kelly said fishing for information.

I felt as though she didn't believe Lucas' story about helping me any more than I did.

"He fixed it did he? Well, I guess Sebastian doesn't need any help from me then. I didn't think the crane would be up and running so fast Sebastian," shot Lucas accusingly.

"Kelly was a big help, Lucas. She knows a lot about the equipment she operates. You can't get much past her," I said defensively.

"Stop it you too. I'm right here. You're right Sebastian, you can't get much past me so stop trying to. You were both so obviously a blind man would be able to read between the double-space lines that you're leaving," Kelly snapped indignantly.

"Lucas, VI-Count came down today," I said gravely.

"What do you mean he came down today? VI-Count never comes down to the lower parts unless there's an assembly, but even then he's on an elevated platform," said Lucas in disbelief.

"Exactly! That's what tipped me off something big is going on here. Something bigger than a broken crane," said Kelly.

"Lucas, I told Kelly about how I was supposed to keep the crane in disrepair. About VI-Count bringing in the Corp." I said with a tremble in my voice that I tried to hide without any success.

"It's OK Sebastian. Kelly knows about me already," Lucas said reassuringly.

"She does! Why didn't she tell me? Why didn't you tell me? I have been worried all day that Lucas would be furious at me!" I said anger swelling within my chest.

This seemed to be information I could not handle at the moment. I was already dealing with so much. Learning that I went through all that necessary stress was infuriating!

"I did not want to get involved, but now it seems that I have no choice. I told Stella that I would watch after you, and I knew about Lucas and Toby. They were to watch over you and protect you as well. But that's all I knew. That's why when Lucas came down here I knew it was something serious," Kelly said soothingly.

"So are you going to help us?" Lucas asked gently his blue eyes pleading for help.

He knew as well as I did that we needed Kelly at this point to get the crane back in submission. I can see from the way Lucas looked at Kelly that he trusted her as well. I wondered if he tried to get her to help in the past and she refused. There seemed to be a whole other story here. Another piece of the puzzle. I wondered if I would be filled in anytime soon.

That didn't seem to be the case at this time because Lucas said we had to come up with a plan and quickly. Kelly and I knew that VI-Count was personally going to come down to check on the project later in the day. We had to be ready. We had to prove to him that the crane was up and running again.

Chapter 18

"I'm in" Said Kelly.

"Glad to have you with us," said Lucas with a wide grin.

" I better leave before VI-Count returns. It probably won't look good with me here. See you later. Be safe. And Kelly. I know you don't want to get involved. Sorry for that, but thanks for your help" said Lucas appreciatively.

"I'm not doing it for you or your cause. I'm only doing this for Sebastian," Kelly said firmly.

"Understood," said Lucas.

He looked hurt as he turned and walked away shoulders slumped like a child who was told he could no longer play.

Once Lucas was out of view Kelly turned to me and said to me"We better get to work. I have to have something before VI-Count and Lord Byron come back to see if the crane has been repaired."

Without another word, Kelly hopped up into the crane and got to work. She didn't call in the rest of the crew since there were only a couple of

hours remaining in the workday. By the time they would have gotten there and set up, it would have been time to break down for the day. She just
moved some beams in place getting the staging area set for tomorrow when the real work would begin. Kelly climbed down from the cab and turned to me. Fatigue and sorrow were written across
her face.

"Are you ok?" I asked gently as she came up beside me for a drink of water and a bit of much-needed rest.

"This is a lot for me, Sebastian. It's a lot to try to process. There's a lot of damage that's been done I just don't wanna get into it," said Kelly softly.

"What happened between you and Lucas?" I asked.

"It was a long time ago Sebastian. It's complicated," she said trying to get me off the subject.

"Why do adults always say that? It's just not fair. Just because I'm younger doesn't mean I can't handle complicated. Right now things are more than complicated but look I'm here, handling it. It's obvious that Lucas likes you and that you like him. It was clear that he was happy that you were going to help. It seemed like he has wanted your help for a long time," I said indignantly.

"You're right. I'm sorry. You're not a little kid anymore I need to stop treating you that way. I just forget sometimes. Although I shouldn't. I see a smart young man in front of me now. You're 16 right? Ready to take on the world?" Kelly said with a sly smile.

"Yes I'm 16 and I know I'm not a man but I'm not some little kid either. I don't want to take on the world I just wanna understand. So much of my life has been a lie an allusion and I'm tired of it. I can't take another person especially when I care about lying to me. I need to have some clarity so I know where I'm standing. Because right now Kelly I'm scared and I'm lost. I'm so lost. I feel like I might not be able to make my way back to reality. As soon as I feel like I'm getting a bit of understanding I feel like a curveball is thrown into my face. And I'm left spiraling again unable to find my way back to the surface for air.

155

I'm drowning. Please tell me" I pleaded
desperately.

Hoping that Kelly would open up and let me
in. I knew she needed to talk as much as I needed
to understand.

"Lucas and I were going to get married 13
years ago. It was right before the rebels started to
gather that he proposed. I was so happy. Your
father introduced me to Lucas. He was a welder,
one of the best! He was a part of a key team. But
then the rebels started to gather. The Corp was
gaining more and more control and had become
a monopoly. They were cruel and overworked
their people. They had guards who acted as
foremen. They were unforgiving man. They were
called the Patrol. Danny and Hank were two of
the worst." Said Kelly.

"Wait did you say Danny and Hank, like
Danny and Hank the Watchman?" I asked
stunned.

"One and the same. VI-Count recruited him.
He assured us that they were going to protect us
and they were unhappy with the way the Corp
did things," Kelly explained, "But your father and
Lucas were smart. They avoided Danny and Hank.

Some were careless and got caught not working so they were fired. The Corp. was the only company left to work for. So ones who were fired couldn't buy things or care for themselves anymore. The Corp knew that they were the only company that one could work for. They knew they could get away with treating people any way that they wanted it. Some even died at the plant from unsafe working conditions. Some died from sheer exhaustion. Toby recruited your father and mother along with Shawna's parents," Kelly said trailing off, the memory seemed too painful for her to continue.

"And Lucas?" I ask slowly.

"Right, Lucas. He tried to convince me that it would be better to join the rebellion. I was scared it was all so confusing. It was so hard to know what was up and what was down. Add on top of that people starving and suffering so terribly. We have lost Edwin, Shay, Alex, Gina, Lao, and many others. Some had children. They were so young. VI-Count was offering to take their children and protect them from the Corp. So they wouldn't lose their lives like their parents did. We believed VI-Count and we trusted him." She said.

"Tyler, Maddy, and Dimitri's parents, all of them," I said mournfully.

"Yes, and many more. Your friend Shawna. Her mother Maya was one of the rebel leaders. Her husband was a very smart man. He did not want to fight or join the rebels. He didn't want to leave Shawna behind. It was so sweet he called her by this pet name Tigres. She was already so much like her mom. Maya said that she wasn't going to allow the Corp to break her daughter like they had so many before. Malcolm wanted to run. He convinced Maya to join him. She loved Shawna and did not wanna leave her child either but she felt like she didn't have much of a choice. They went into hiding. Lucas and I brought them supplies for a while. A watchman named Brutus…"

I cut Kelly off to ask "Wait, Brutus, he's one of the watchmen. He's the one who turned in Toby"

"Yes, one and the same. Like I said he's a very cruel man. He went to the hiding place and confronted Malcolm and Maya. Shawna stayed hidden. Maya told them they were no longer going to work for the Corp. There was a bit of a scuffle and Malcolm ended up getting knocked unconscious. He needed a few stitches on his forehead. While Maya was off to the side trying to stop the bleeding another man came into the door. It was Lord Byron. He told Maya he could protect Shawna from the Corp by taking her to VI-Count. He told her that it wasn't too late. But they would have to tell her where they had hidden her. Maya did what she felt like she had to do. She was backed into a corner with her husband knocked unconscious on the floor next to her bleeding. She told Lord Byron where Shawna was hidden. Maya and Malcolm have not seen Shawna since. Your mother did not want the same thing to happen to you. Your father was already on board. Since your father was a leader of one of the rebel groups they convinced Lucas to join. He was more than willing. Emotions were running so high and everyone was so tired of being treated so cruelly. I felt like everyone was being so blinded. I did not want to be a part of anyone's downfall." said Kelly reflectively, as if the past was playing in front of her eyes as she was recalling it to me.

Her facial expressions matched the agony she must have gone through. It hurt my heart to

159

see her suffer so. Having tragic things from 12 1/2 years ago brought to the surface just to relive them. It seemed to be a necessary evil at this time but it was still so difficult to watch.

"He chose the rebellion over you?" I asked her gently reality dawning on me.

"That's why you told him you weren't doing this for him. Because the choice he made 12 1/2 years ago," I said already knowing the answer

"I was beyond hurt Sebastian. I didn't understand what was going on. On top of that pain. My own sister told me she was going to leave and abandon her own son, my nephew. My four-year-old defenseless nephew. There's not a large enough word in the English language to define what was going on inside me at that time. I was blinded by VI-Count and what felt to be at that time a betrayal. His offer seemed like the only way out. And I have been blind all these years. It's a blow to the pride to learn that you have been fooled and the people you have been mad at for so long may have been right the entire time and at least some ways," Kelly said mournfully tears pooling in the corner of her eyes.

"But Lucas is in the Dome. He has always been in the Dome," trying to wrap my mind around that fact. I tried to keep the confusion out of my voice but I don't think it was very convincing.

"Yes, Lucas is in the Dome. Toby and Lucas were to come into the Doom undercover," Kelly said.

I already knew that part but I didn't want to interrupt her again and miss the chance to have details added to fill in the gaps in my mind…

She continued "The damage has been done between Lucas and I. My heart was broken I didn't feel like I could trust him. He is no longer the man who proposed to me. We went our separate ways. Although throughout the years he has tried to get me to see VI-Count for who he really was. But I've been blinded…"

I cut Kelly off again I couldn't help myself

"Blinded by an illusion that VI-Count offered us," I added indignantly defending my aunt.

We could not blame ourselves, that would only keep us locked in and give VI-Count more power over us. I refuse to let Kelly do that.

"Yes blinded by the illusion that he offered us. That's a good way to put it. I feel so broken Sebastian. How am I supposed to help and protect you, when I am not sure which way is up?" Kelly said truly perplexed her eyes pleading with me.

"Anyway, we still had to communicate about you. He always asked the same questions and I would give him a report. It was weird to say the lease. Having someone you cared for so deeply and shared everything with then turned into a cold yes and no conversation. Like a light switch was turned off, like what we shared never even existed. It was so empty and lonely." Kelly said sadness dripping from her every word.

"I don't see that. You both still love each other. Your cheeks both turn red and you both get a little funny acting around each other. You both even seem a bit younger when you're together" I said trying not to sound too corny.

I think it was having the desired effect because a smile crept across her face and the mood lighted a little.

"Easy now are you trying to call me old," Kelly said fully grinning now.

It was good to see her smile. The fatigue and sorrowful look was not a good look on her. It even made her blue eyes look as if they were fading. I hated to see her like this. It was almost more than my heart could handle. Just then all our smiles melted away for VI-Count and Lord Byron walked into the East Wing.

Chapter 19

"I can see the crane has been running this afternoon," said VI-Count with disturbing and uncomfortable pleasure in his voice.

"Yes sir, Sebastian was able to fix it. I have prepared the staging area for tomorrow. We will be ready to go first thing in the morning," Kelly said confidently.

"Excellent. Then our expansion project will be on track despite our setback," said VI-Count confidently.

"I am sure we will not have any further setbacks of this nature, will we Sebastian?" Questioned Lord Byron with a snarl, that made the blood drain from my face.

"No sir!" I said as confidently and innocently as I could.

"We will detain you no further," VI-Count stated abruptly ending the conversation.

I wondered how someone without people skills could rise to the position that he holds today. After VI-Count and Lord Byron left Kelly and I both let out a huge sigh. I believe we are both holding our breath during the encounter.

"What now?" I asked.

" I am not sure to be honest. We have to hold off from any crane issues for a while. We'll have to find another way to delay the project," Kelly said which is a mischievous grin.

That look made me glad that Kelly was on our side and not on VI-Counts! We went back to our quarters to clean up for dinner. It was a quiet walk back to the South Wing. Kelly nodded slightly and I continued toward my room. I was ready to clean up and shower. Hoping the shower will be able to wash off not just the dirt but also the day and all that came with it. I wasn't sure what to do next so I simply got dressed in my gray uniform and sat at my desk in the center of the room. Allowing my mind to drift this way and that. It felt good to rest and to be able to relax. Using the term relax very loosely. My jaw ached probably from clenching my teeth together so much today. I never noticed that I had done that before. It was probably the stress of the encounter with VI-Count and Lord Byron this afternoon. Along with my intense

worry about how Lucas was going to respond to the fact that I told Kelly about the mission. The memory stirred a bit of anger. My feelings twisted and riled together. Something good did come out of the day. I did learn that Kelly was my aunt. It
was nice to know that I not only had Shawna but I also had a piece of my mom here with me. It seemed to make all of this a bit easier somehow.

As I was starting to rise from the horribly uncomfortable seat in my desk I noticed a small piece of paper drifting down from the vent above. I reached for it slowly not sure if I even wanted to read the words. I've learned that I could not turn back once I allowed the knowledge to my brain. Uncertainty filled my mind. My hands shook as I debated with myself. I knew it was a losing battle. I would have to read it. But I didn't have to read it alone. I can read it with Shawna. Should I take the chance? What if I couldn't safely share it with her? What if someone else was to read it? I quickly shove the note in my pocket before interrogating myself any longer. As I headed to the center I could smell the same odor that filled the Dome around this time every evening. Not a pleasing mouthwatering smell but one that had only one explanation. Potatoes. Again.

   We tended to eat not out of pleasure but more for survival here in the Dome. I was so furious at the greedy corporations for destroying the planet wiping out the possibilities of ever tasting a lobster again. I had to stop this rant, I would take my frustration out on the potato I was about to have.

   I walked over the bridge that took me over top of the grassy running track. Pausing to notice Tyler and Lucas running side-by-side. I feel like I should join them maybe getting some of this nervous energy out. It was a peaceful evening. The fleeting sun was setting over the West wing. This is what we call the golden hour. All seemed to be content. The atrium is beautifully illuminated. What was left of the remaining sun glistening off the waxy leaves of a banana tree overhead helped to calm my nervousness. I took the time to breathe deeply for the first time and what felt like forever. I could hear Maddy and Dimitri laughing over at the ping-pong table. Dimitri was pretty much always there when he wasn't welding eating or sleeping. I saw Kelly on the grass with the book probably trying to escape to calm her mind from the day in the wound that was torn open. Aki was on a bench not far off. He seemed to be looking observing and drinking up everyone else's actions or movements. It was a bit eerie, to be honest.

"Hey," came a familiar voice from behind.

"Hey yourself," I replied.

"Rough day?" She asked.

"The understatement of the century" I retorted.

"How about yours?" I asked.

"Uneventful. Which I am relieved about. Tell me about your day," she said concerned.

"We better sit down this will take a minute," I said.

We walked on the bridge that crossed over the little creek turning left at the edge then when no one was looking we jumped and sat under the bridge. It was a peaceful spot. One Shawna and I have always loved. I filled her in on my day and she listened quietly. Even her expressions were
quiet. I wasn't sure what was going through her

mind as I filled her in about Kelly being my aunt. The unhealed wounds between her and my mom as well as Lucas. And how Kelly now knows about VI-Count. When I finished she still didn't speak for a while which was unusual for Shawna. But I was patient because I knew it was a lot to process. Well patient for about two minutes.

"Well?" I asked, patiently.

"I always thought Kelly had your mom's eyes and now I guess we know why," was all that she said.

I could tell she needed some time to allow in all the connections in her mind. As we were looking out we both noticed Tyler and Lucas as they ran by. Lucas gave the slightest of glances our way. I could see why my parents had chosen Lucas. He was keenly observant always. I didn't think a fly could buzz by without his notice. He was so patient and even-keeled. I had never seen him overreact. Then I noticed Aki. He seems to be watching Kelly. Shawna must've noticed it too because she spoke up.

"Do you think Aki knows about, you know Lucas?" Shawna asked sheepishly.

"I don't know," was all I could say because I truly did not know.

Then the dinner alert sounded and we all joined the lineup. I guarantee prison food has more of a taste and variety than we received here in the Dome. But we all agreed to eat because we were so hungry. Some of our work assignments were tough and we needed the calories. It wasn't because of enjoyment that we ate that was for sure. All was quiet in the center except for the clinking of silverware on our metal bowls. I guess it's hard to make food look appealing when everything you eat looks like it is for animals. Like dog bowls. Everything was metal. Metal cups, metal bowls, metal trays, and of course metal silverware. It seemed to be absorbed into the food as well. Dimitri asked Shawna if she would like to have a match of ping-pong after dinner but she said she was too exhausted and needed to get some rest. Lucas spoke up quickly and added that he thought we should all get rest. We were all a bit caught off guard by Lucas's announcement until we heard what came next over the loudspeakers.

"Tomorrow all are to report to the Dome at 5 AM for a briefing and an update on the expansion. We will need everyone fully rested and alert so please head directly to your quarters after dinner," crackled the loudspeaker.

We all looked at each other in concern. That means VI-Count wants more support and wants to see how we can speed up the construction. Panic filled the room. I dreaded the day that would follow.

My mind and body were restless not wanting the needed rest to be met in this fashion. The sleep-robbing sheets were busily at work. My pillows seem flatter than ever. The air seems stale. I felt as though I would suffocate if I didn't get fresh air. The walls seem to be closing in. I shot up gasping for air, overwhelmed and overcome with anxiety about the next day. What was I going to do? A thought was nagging at the back of my brain. How did Lucas know before the announcement? How could he have gotten confidential information before it was made public to the lower class? As my thoughts drifted to Kelly, my breathing slowed. I pictured her blue eyes, my mother's eyes. Her rich complexion is

171

like that and my mother. The thought that she fought for me. That she cared. My mind shifted with ease to my parents. No longer angry at them.Reality sunk in that this could not have been easy for them. It must've been a very difficult decision. One that came about because of so much loss and fear.

They feared that same future for me and they tried to protect me the best way they knew how. At the time with what seemed to be protection anyway. Handing me over to VI-Count was what they felt was the only solution. I pictured my mother longing for me her son. It had my heart ache. My father missed out on my many milestones as I developed my ability. I never before

felt this empty void hungry for relief. Reaching for comfort, love, and support. A void that can only be filled by my mom and dad. With fond memories now gently tickling in my mind filling in the needed warmth nourishing that void. Nourished enough to allow me to fall asleep. I never again wanted to go to the infirmary or see Maxine or Logan. Now that memories were returning I cannot imagine them robbing them for me again. I refuse! I will cling to them as life itself a stabilizer for my mind and heart. As all the deceit continues to manifest itself I need my memories to keep me stable, I will not let them go.

Chapter 20

The next morning I jolted upright at 4:15 AM. I longed for more sleep. My eyes were heavy battling me to remain closed. My legs and arms were unyielding. Come on I said to myself. We have to get up. This is a mandatory meeting. Everyone must be there. I pulled up my boots and staggered to a little kitchenette to grab a muffin. I stopped and looked at the brainwashing vitamins. I realized that I needed to do something with the vitamins that would make it seem like I had been taking them so as not to raise any suspicion. My hand quickly snatched them off the old warped off-white countertop. I counted out what I was thinking to be the number of days that I had missed. At first accidentally but now very much on purpose. I wrapped them in a small piece of cloth and threw them into the deep dark pit. Hopefully, they will dissolve before the big cleaning comes again. I was told of life outside of Dome a time when people had toilets that flushed with water. Freshwater to flush down human waste. That was crazy. Especially when we learned that in some countries people had to walk miles each day just to get a supply of water for that day. It seems like such a waste of resources. No wonder water became so scarce.

What about water for the outsiders? Water is so severely contaminated. I wondered what the outsiders had to do to find fresh water. Did they have purifiers as we have inside the Dome? Even so, water was precious. We had to use it very sparingly. We had toothbrushes with liquid toothpaste that could be used without water. We had metal disinfectant caps to clean them after use. We had waterless shampoo and conditioner. We could only shower two times a week and only a two-minute intervals. Our laundry was clean with steam instead of gallons of water. It was difficult.

I did not even want to think about 95 more adults moving into the Dome. What will happen then? With the vitamin situation handled I grabbed my muffin. I gobbled it down. Maybe blueberry not sure. One day I told myself I was going to be able to sit down and chew my food and maybe even be able to tell what flavor it was. But now I have bigger things to think about than the flavor of my muffin. Now that I had control over my body I was out the door headed for the auditorium. Shawna jogged up beside me.

"Hey," she said.

"Hey yourself," I said in return.

That was all we dared to say. The South wing was full of Lower-class members working their way towards the auditorium. I heard a couple grumbling to each other about how the assembly was just going to tell us to work harder and faster. He didn't get to finish his statement though he was quieted by the woman next to him. It was Kelly. She caught my eye and gave me a slight smile. She had a bit of a twinkle in her eye when she saw me. She was smart and others would be wise to listen to her.

"We can't work any harder. I am already working 10-hour shifts," grumbled Aki.

"I wish I were only working 10 hours. I have been working 12-hour shifts for three months. I am mixing so much concrete that I'm even doing it in my sleep. I am eating it for breakfast, lunch, and dinner. It is wearing away at my teeth," complained Jonas.

"My blisters have blisters from getting nuts and bolts ready for the impact guns," lamented Sam.

"You all need to keep your voice down. If Lord Byron hears you all there is going to be trouble" spat Lucas trying to talk so sense into the crowd.

They were tired, I get it, but we all had to be careful. If the others only realized how much... I noticed he gave Kelly a warm smile but she simply looked away. I wondered why and how after all this time living under the same roof for 12 1/2 years, how come they hadn't been able to work out their differences? I mean you can't love someone so much that you want to marry them then just not, right?? It was beyond me. I mean here my parents gave me up but I wasn't holding a grudge I just found out. Kelly knows VI-Count is a liar. Why isn't she forgiving Lucas?

Shawna tapped me on the shoulder and gave the slightest hand gesture to her lips. It was Lord Byron. He was watching intently making sure everyone was accounted for. I saw everyone but the Morris family. I was hoping they did not have to attend since they had a small child. They have been able to be on work leave for the past two weeks. This is the first baby to be born in the Dome. Which is odd now that I think about it… There are a number of married couples that could have children. I would have to remember to bring this up with Lucas later. I can see the back of Dimitri, Tyler, and Maddy's heads a little ways ahead.

We all filed in through the steel double doors into the auditorium. It was nice I didn't feel so claustrophobic even with 250 people in the room. This was because of the glass panels that covered the roof above the platform. This provided
natural lighting. The auditorium had wood walls instead of metal. This helped to carry sound even to those all the way in the back of the room. Everyone seems to be alert despite the unnatural hour to be awake.

"Good Morning and thank you all for coming. We are glad to discuss our progress regards the expansion. I want to thank you all for all your hard work. We could not accomplish such great feet if were not for all of your efforts. I am grateful. Unfortunately, due to a crane being out of commission for three weeks, we have fallen behind. Supplies are prepped and ready. Welders Lucas, Dimitri, and Aki we will need you to put in some overtime on the expansion site past the greenhouse. Kelly will be working a long shift as well to try to catch up. Jonas, we need you to work overtime as well to keep them supplied with concrete to get the beams in place. Sam you and Sally will be on bolt duty. I am sorry to inconvenience you all but this is for the best of everyone in the Dome. We will all benefit greatly from your hard work and self-sacrifice. We will still be on target and finish up the expansion before the ice storms hit. Soon we will even enjoy foods other than potatoes." At this, a cheer broke out through the crowd. The thought of some other food besides potatoes was too much to hold in. It seemed to lessen the blow of all the overtime for the crowd. This was a crowd of people that have worked hard all their lives. VI-Count told them thank you a few times. Something the Corp never did. They trusted him, believing they would get something in return, believing that they were working together with the same good purpose. How wrong they were. With their own hands, they were preparing the way for the entrance of a brutal enemy, the Corp.

Chapter 21

I watched the crowd's reaction to VI-Count's words turn from outrage and sheer exhaustion to one of hope and longing for something better. I had to admit that VI-Count was

good. He may not be a people person, but he sure knew how to steer people's emotions and thoughts. It was plain to see how he could've swayed the parents not so long ago as well as Kelly and others believe in him. My heart went out to those who were bamboozled. Then my face flushed because I too had been willing to go along with him as well.

My thoughts drifted to Kelly. As an adult and now knowing the truth about VI-Count. I wondered how today's assembly was going to affect her. She too must feel so awful. As I scanned the crowded room I saw Lucas looking over at Kelly. His usually kind and gentle face was pained. I quickly shifted my gauge to see tears streaming down Kelly's face. My breath caught in my chest. It hurt me to see Kelly in so much pain.

It even bothered me to see Lucas so hurt now that I have gotten to know him and all he has done for us. The revelation has been hard, more than hard. I have never seen Kelly cry. I saw Lucas start to move towards her but stopped suddenly. Aki was there beside Kelly asking if she was ok while handing her a tissue. His brown eyes were eager to gain Kelly's affection. He seemed almost happy
to see her in this state, hoping to prey on her vulnerability. Holding onto her hand a little too long for my liking. I knew this was not easy for Lucas. Now that I knew of their past it was more evident than ever the love that Lucas still had for her. I could see the protection he wanted to offer Kelly in his rigid intense body language at the sight of Aki comforting her instead of him.
If looks could kill, Aki wouldn't make it far.

  Something else drew my attention away from the scene before me. Up on the top level of the Dome, I saw Louis stealthily creeping along the steel walkway. She had a manila file folder in her right hand. She was taking a somewhat complicated, seemingly erratic path. At closer inspection, it looked as if she was purposefully walking in that fashion. Shawna came up from behind. She must have noticed my gaze.

"Cameras, she's avoiding cameras," Shawna said conspiratorially.

"How do you know?" I asked wondering how she knew the location of the cameras on the upper level.

Shawna would not have access to that information.

"It stands to reason. VI-Count would protect the upper level since his quarters, his office, and that of the other Nobles are up there. It's like the brain of the Dome," Shawna said.

"And now would be the perfect time to pick at that brain since everyone is at the assembly," I said, clearly seeing Shawna's point. I was rewarded for my quick insight by a slight smile from Shawna pride filling her eyes. As Shawna and I were watching Louis I wondered how she got away with not being at the assembly today. All Nobles were supposed to be here. There was a quick sharp poke at my back, as well as Shawna's, followed by a clipped instruction given by Lucas.

"Put your head down. You're putting Louis in

danger by calling attention to her," Lucas said gruffly along with a sharp look.

We both quickly obeyed.

"What is she doing?" Shawna asked unable to conceal her intrigue.

"I am not sure exactly," said Lucas honestly.

"Louis is how you knew about the announcement for today's assembly, isn't it?" I questioned.

"Yes," Lucas said not wanting to give too much more detail.

"Doesn't VI-Count and the others realize she isn't here?" asked Shawna before I could.

"No, she has been in some trouble as of late and is supposed to be in lockdown, confined to her room," Lucas said with a conspiratorial smile.

"You don't have anything to do with that do you?" Shawna asked amused.

"Hush! It's not safe for Louis or me to continue this conversation. Just know she's a good guy well technically girl," Lucas said proudly.

Our conversation was interrupted by the loudspeaker with the announcement,

"Time for everyone to return back to work,"

The murmurs and complaints I would have expected did not come. Instead, everyone was eager to get to work. Sam and Sally were even excitedly chatting away about new recipes they would be able to try. Jones even joined in saying that it would be nice to mix something other than concrete. Everyone was so busy focusing on the possibility of a bright future, one with more options to eat, and a larger living area. VI-Count's words have stolen all the ability to look past them and blinded almost every one of his motives. There was nothing else any of us could do at this moment that would not give rise to suspicion other than go back to work. Unsure of what to do next.

Chapter 22

As I left the assembly I felt more perplexed than ever. How could everything still be the same for almost everyone around me yet for me personally be so different? I feel like I am constantly battling for freedom of my mind and thoughts as cognitive dissonance keeps whispering to me. I know that VI-Count is a liar and a fraud. But my narrow perception of reality up until now and for so long has been that VI-Count is our protector.

He is a good guy. As my mind wavered back and forth I was really beginning to run low on hope. I honestly didn't see any way out of this complex and complicated situation. As the fog of those life-shattering events started to clear I wondered how it was that I had never seen certain things before. I mean you would think that someone who was your protector would make you feel safe and secure. Instead, VI-Count had always been creepy to me, with his ghostly white hair, pale skin, and menacing stare that made the hairs on the back of my neck stand up. And that scar on his right cheek distorts his already frightening face. His unusually tall statue was also very intimidating.

He wasn't bulky by no means but he was very fit. No pushover that's for sure. Added to that, he doesn't even really like people. At the assemblies, his tone is more controlling and domineering than caring or protecting making you feel like you didn't have any other choice but to listen to him. It was more like listen to me or get out. Shawna came up beside me.

"Man that was disturbing!" She said will a creeped-out look on her face.

"Tell me about it!" I agreed, equally perplexed.

"Everyone's like vulnerable trusting sheep following after a man who is leading them to the slaughter. They're just happily following along completely unaware of his cruel intentions," Shawn said mournfully.

A heavy cloud covered her normal chipper expression. Shawna almost tackled me knocking me back against the wall. I was so caught off guard. Shawna was not a hugger whatsoever. I could tell all the events of the last few days were weighing down on her. But to be honest I wasn't sure what to do with the sudden display of warmth and affection.

Not having my parents around for the last 12 years probably explained why I wasn't really much of a huggy touchy person. Same with Shawna. I finally settled on wrapping my arms around her shoulders as she cried. I didn't say a word. The fact that Shawna was in this state was almost too much for me. I allowed a few tears to escape my eyes as well. It was nice not to feel so alone and to know that I was not the only one that was struggling. But to be honest, seeing Shawna like this made what little hope I had disappeared into oblivion. After a few moments, she pulled away. Her eyes were swollen red and puffy. My gray suit turned dark by the puddle of tears as well as probably snot that she left on my shirt. She pulled a handkerchief out of her pocket. It was a pretty blue color, silky looking. She noticed me looking at it.

"It was my mom's. She gave it to me to dry my tears the night we went into hiding. I was so little and so afraid. I have always kept it with me since then," Shawn spoke so softly it was barely audible.

She looked so vulnerable and small in that moment. I hated seeing her this way, I wanted to fix, to repair any damage as well as hurt that had been done to my friend. Normally I would make a comment like, "I hope you have washed" it or something silly. But the situation was too heavy for that kind of joking and I knew it. She had never told me about the handkerchief this was the first time I'd ever seen it or even learned of his existence. I didn't even know Shawna to be a sentimental type. So I settled with a simple question.

"You have kept it all this time?" I said.

A simple "yes" was all that she could muster.

"How is it that moments, small periods of time, even something as small as seconds can completely shatter your world without remorse. Abandoning you to try to piece together the remains. Only it's impossible because so much was destroyed that you can't even discern or make out anything that's left," Shawna stated more than asked.

"Shawna, I know this seems hopeless. I feel it too. But we need to figure out a way to piece ourselves together so that we can help each other, as well as the others. We have come this far. It's too far to give up now. Besides our parents are out there. They were fooled just like us as well as the others in the Dome. We have to help them before it's too late. Who knows what VI-Count will do once the Corp's in the Dome? One thing is for sure, I don't think they will want the likes of the Lower class members around." I said solemnly.

"Sebastian you're a genius," Shawna shot up, all sadness and fatigue replaced with a sharp burst of energy.

"Yes, we already know that but how exactly am I a genius in this case?" I asked very confused.

Shawna has never called me a genius before, many other names but genius definitely wasn't one of them.

" VI-Count has used the Lower class these last 12 years to build a Dome. To repair it and get it supplied. He needed workers to do this. It's not something he could've done on his own or even with the help of the Nobles. You know that neither of those groups has touched a tool once in their entire lives. He was never going to allow the Lower class members to move up or to learn more. It was all part of the bait to get them, and us to

help. These last 12 years we've been working not for ourselves or for our futures. We've been slaving for VI-Count and what he wants. He doesn't care about us. He's going to get rid of the Lower class members before they even know about the Corp. moving in, I'm sure of it," Shawna said with such confidence that I could not help but believe her myself.

"That would protect him from having to deal with an uprising or a rebellion," I said in agreement.

"That's probably why he has been so tight-lipped and secretive, even more so than before. Because he is so close to moving the Corp in and he doesn't want anyone to find out because that would ruin everything," Shawna said.

"We need to tell the others," I said.

"We need to tell the others what?" Questioned Lord Byron.

That snake! Shawna and I froze, afraid of what he may have overheard. Lord Byron was no fool. Unlike VI-Count he was short only about my height. But what he lacked in height he made up for in bulk. For that reason, everyone gave him a wide berth. If his size didn't scare you then his piercing steel gray eyes would.

It felt like he was cutting right through to all your innermost thoughts without you even having to say a word. It made it even more difficult to try to come up with a lie. I could see the vein in his forehead swell. His frustration building. He didn't like to be kept waiting.

"I can't wait to tell the others about how excited we are to be so close to finishing the expansion. VI-Count's speech this morning was so moving," Shawna lied.

"Me too! I can't wait until something other than potato soup, potato cakes, potato bread, potato fries, and baked potatoes are served." I added.

"Ok, Ok I get the point. Stop blubbering and wasting my time! Get back to your assignments!" Lord Byron shot back.

Shawna and I looked at each other relieved. He must not have heard our conversation. At least it seemed that he didn't. We had to be more cautious. We needed to get our emotions under control. They were causing us to be sloppy. We had to get our head in the game as the saying goes. We set off to work promising to meet up later.

Chapter 23

Since the crane was operational I was given a new assignment. I needed to repair the concrete mixer. This was no small-scale mixer. We actually had two cement trucks because a small-scale mixer would never be able to keep up. Lucas and Aki along with Dimitri helped to convert the truck from diesel to electric. We needed to remove any exhaust fumes. They would prove deadly for all in the Dome since we did not have open ventilation.

I was pretty sure this was sabotage that I was going to run into today with the concrete mixer. I am glad they only took down one truck not both. That would've been sloppy and drawn way too much attention. A certain amount of repair was necessary and even required. Standard wear and tear as well as a need for maintenance and replacing parts was normal. Jonas and Rick were our concrete men. It was Jonas's rig was down.

I hated to be in this part of the construction site. The lime in the air from the concrete mix seems to find every possible piece of saliva completely disappeared from existence. It was far from pleasant. It was a bit louder than where the crane was operating because of the constant tumbling of the sand and gravel which seemed to echo off every inch of the glass panels amplifying the ruckus.

Hearing protection was important. Day after day without it could cause loss of hearing. Rick unfortunately did not realize this until the damage had been done. He used to work for the Corp. mixing concrete. Jonas said he lost most of his hearing then. So he didn't see the point of wearing ear protection now. Rick was a great lip reader though. He had keen eyesight and was a true master of what he did. Jonas really respected Rick.

Rick was 25 years Jonas' senior and because of that, he looked to Rick as a father figure. Jonas' own father had died under the greedy hands of the Corp. Worked to death. This really bugged me. Here men like Jonas and Rick had lost so much to the Corp. and they looked to VI-Count as someone to trust. Only if they knew what he had in store for them, for all of us.

195

I wanted to tell Jonas but I didn't want to risk it. He might not believe me. I could not just stand there debating with myself all day. So instead I got to work on fixing the mixer. I did my best to drag out the repair. Jonas said he was going to lie down in the truck and get some sleep. He told me the long hours were wearing him down. You could see it in his face. Jonah was very short only 5' 3". He was very pale looking like a man who had never seen much sunlight in his life. This made the dark circles under his eyes even more pronounced. I told him I would let him know if I had it repaired but assured him it was going to be a few hours. He seemed relieved at the prospect of being able to get some rest since it wouldn't be a quick fix. That helped me to not feel quite so guilty.

As I was looking around I noticed a piece of what looked like aluminum foil tucked down deep into the hydraulic transmission system. I quickly looked around to ensure that no one was paying attention. I stayed tucked into my uncomfortable position and slowly unfolded the foil. As I suspected there was a little piece of paper inside. The note read…

I quickly refolded the note and stuffed it into my shirt pocket. I was not really shocked by this. I never really trusted Aki very much anyway. He didn't seem to really like Lucas very much. I became suspicious thinking that was why VI-Count had Aki working with Lucas. So he could report to him anything that would prove Lucas was involved with the outside. I remembered that Lucas spoke freely with Aki in the past. I wonder if Aki's turning was more recent.

There was a little welding to be done to the supporting wheel system so I went to find Lucas. I peeked into the truck to let Jonas know that I was going to find Lucas but he was snoring so loudly and even had a small puddle of drool on the seat cushion so I figured I better let him be. He sure seemed in need of rest. Frustration again surged through me at the site of seeing this man so used I mistreated.

I found Lucas in the infirmary. He was doing a quick mig weld on one of the steel tables. One of the legs had a crack in the weld. That was the last thing Maxine and Logan wanted was for a patient to lie down on the table and have it collapse
under them causing even more injury. Maxine smiled as she saw me come in.

I hated the infirmary. Besides the fact that Maxine and Logan lied about the injections and vitamins the place also reeked of sanitizing chemicals and latex.

"Sebastian, what brings you here?" Maxine said happily.

"Is it time for your injection Sebastian?" questioned Logan almost excitedly which really got under my skin.

I tried to hide my irritation.

"No, no, not yet. I am here because I need Lucas," I said maybe a little too quickly.

"What for?" asked Lucas.

"A beam on the mixer is broken and needs to be welded," I said.

"OK, I just finished up here. Let me just grab my bag and we will be on our way," said Lucas.

"Great!" I said relieved to get out of there as quickly as possible.

"Sebastian, I looked up your record. It seems we will see you in three days for your injection. Don't forget. We'll also give you your next supply of vitamins," Maxine said cheerfully.

Those creeps! They had absolutely no remorse!

"Ok, see you then," I said through gritted teeth.

When we got into the hallway I quickly told Lucas about the note. He didn't seem surprised.

I had to ask, "Why do I get the impression you already knew that."

"I have seen Aki leaving the Dome from time to time this past two weeks," Lucas said.

"Does he have any idea about you and your involvement?" I asked worried.

"I am not sure to be honest. But I hope not," said Lucas contemplatively.

"I'm trying to stretch this out as long as possible," I reassured Lucas.

"I know, you're doing a good job. I know this is not at all easy," Lucas said reassuringly.

I have not experienced this side of Lucas much so it was a bit of a shock but it was nice. He was right. It is so hard. I feel like a traitor even though I know it's the right thing to do. I asked Lucas what he thought about Shawna's idea about how VI-Count is planning to get rid of the Lower-class members before bringing in the Corp. to avoid an uprising. He told me that was only half of it. He told me that VI-Count is not only going to get rid of the Lower class members from the Dome but that he has also rigged the underground hideout. He plans to blow them up. My parents, Shawna's parents, and all the others outside.

"It's OK Sebastian don't panic they already know. I think that's why they gave us the note. They are telling us Aki is behind it," Lucas said confidently and calmly.

"That must've been what he was up to when he was on the outside then," I said, trying to piece together this ever more difficult puzzle.

"VI-Count probably offered him some type of bribe and Aki readily accepted it not thinking about anyone but himself," Lucas said angrily.

"I worry about Kelly. I see him watching her all the time. It really creeps me out." I said growing concern in my voice.

"I know," Lucas said through gritted teeth.

His face flushed hot with anger. I felt like there may be a bit more to the story here, but I didn't push it.

"What are we gonna do Lucas," I asked.

"We will have to wait and see Sebastian," was all that Lucas said. Then he went to work.

Chapter 24

I was just tightening the last bolt when the door to the cement truck flew open spitting Jonas out! He looked wild-eyed. Is typical pale skin glowing red. His thinning dusty brown hair was fighting over which part of the scalp they should work together to cover resulting in sheer chaos. Adding to the look of a madman was a bunch of deep grooves on his right cheek. Impressions made by the truck seat.

"Sebastian!" Jonas yelled at the top of his lungs.

I was startled and impressed that so much volume could come out of such a man. I was so taken aback that I instantly dropped my wrench. As it bounded off the side of the truck I tried to shout a warning but I could not get my words together fast enough. A few seconds later my wrench contact with Jona's left cheek causing him to cry out in pain as well as shock. Once the wrench was lying on the floor after finishing its assault on Jonas he peed up at me. A bruise forming on his cheek already.

"Watch what you're doing" he shouted annoyed.

"Sorry, you startled me when you came out of the truck yelling," I explained.

"Easy Jonas," Lucas soothed. But Jonas wanted no part of being soothed or calmed down!

"Easy! I just got hit in the face with a wrench and you want me to be easy! On top of that, it's nearly 4:30, meaning I slept through my entire workday!" Jonas fumed.

"I understand you're upset. Sebastian did not drop the wrench on purpose. You startled him when you jumped out of the truck. To be honest you scared me!" Lucas said with a hearty laugh.

Jonas took a second to peer at himself in the truck's mirror. He jolted back at the site of himself. Understanding fell into place and he relaxed. He licked his hands and rubbed them through his hair trying to bring some type of order. He wiped the traces of drool off his right cheek and then gently rubbed the lump on his left cheek from the wrench incident. His complexion was returning to its normal pale tone instead of glowing red.

"Sorry. I saw the clock and I panicked. I didn't want to get in trouble again. I have to be able to reach my day's work quota," Jonas said meekly.

"Have you been in trouble recently?" asked Lucas concerned.

Jonas was a hard worker. Even with the hectic schedule and lack of sleep, he didn't really complain. He gave his best. I could tell Lucas was upset by what Jonas said. Lucas was biting the bottom left corner of his lip. I didn't know if he even realized that he did this but I noticed it when he was deep in thought or was contemplating something. His blue eyes were mournful and I could see his struggle. Finally, he began to speak.

"What did you get in trouble for?" Lucas asked cautiously.

"VI-Count came down here and told me that Rick was putting out twice as much work as me and that I needed to keep pace or I would find myself in a different situation," Jonas said sadly.

His cheeks were reddening as he was speaking.

"A different situation? What do you think he meant?" Lucas questioned.

"I'm not sure but from the look on VI-Count's face, I know it was not a good alternative. That's why I freaked out. It's not fair because Rick has been at this a lot longer than me. He was able to keep up with the Corp and their ridiculous schedule! But this has even seemed to age him. There's more and more salt in his salt-and-pepper hair each day. And you know what else, it's weird because Rick told me the schedule we have now and what VI-Count is asking of us is almost as bad as the Corp," Jonas set conspiratorially.

"I agree something is up!" Lucas said while really watching Jonas for a response.

I feel like he is testing the waters to see if Jonas would be someone safe to confide in. It was so tricky to know who was safe and who would simply turn on you. Lucas knew this that's why he was being so cautious.

"I know it's for a good cause but if it kills us in the process all of this will be for nothing. No one will be here to enjoy it except maybe VI-Count and Lord Byron." Jonas murmured.

"You definitely have a point there!" Lucas added.

I was surprised that he didn't go on and explain to Jonas what was happening. I would've. Rick came up behind Lucas and put his hand on his shoulder.

"Hey Lucas, how are the repairs going?" Rick asked.

"Almost there! I will have it finished up in about five minutes," Lucas said confidently.

"That's good. I need my sidekick back. It's not easy trying to do the work of two men!" Rick said with a warm smile directed toward Jonas.

"Sorry Rick, I don't know what happened," Jonas said guiltily.

"There is nothing for you to be sorry for Jonas. Trucks break down all the time. Things like this happen. It's out of our control. I'm just grateful we have good, no great mechanics and welders like our Sebastian and Lucas here. I know they are working hard to get you back online," Rick said proudly.

His hazel eyes reflected how he felt about Jonas. You can see the fatherly care and protective nature that Rick had for Jonas. This speech he made made me feel like crawling under a rock. I may be a good mechanic but how good of a person am I stretching out a five-minute job into an all-day one? Causing anxiety for Jonas and an extra workload for Rick. Lucas and I didn't deserve this praise. I could tell Rick's words were eating Lucas alive. He was way more guilty than I was. This could not be easy for him. Lucas was a very hard worker who took pride in his work.

"At least you were able to get some sleep, I'm jealous!" said Rick with a chuckle.

I liked to see Rick laugh. He had deep wrinkles from age, but all that he had been through in life was not seen when he laughed. He had the ability to light up a room. Most people in the Dome enjoyed being around him. He always says the trick to not allowing others to crush or control you is to be happy, no matter what they try to do. Never let them take away your ability to laugh and smile. Because when you give them that, then they have won. I admired Rick because he didn't just say things, he lived by what he said. It showed me that our size has nothing to do with our ability to overcome obstacles, it's really our heart that counts, and as far as Rick was concerned, he had the biggest heart of all of us! It was truly amazing because Rick had been worked like a dog but he had said it wasn't quite as bad as the Corp. He had worked under their harsh conditions for years.

Not many came as tough as Rick. Many men died under less. He would be a strong addition to the cause but Lucas didn't say a word. I was going to have to talk with him after this. I just didn't understand his reasoning. Why was he holding back? We finished up and said our goodbyes to Jonas and Rick. We all went to get cleaned up. On the way back to our quarters when Jonas and Rick were gone I asked Lucas.

"Why didn't you tell Jonas?" He seems to want answers. And Rick he's so strong he will provide a lot to the group," I said confidently feeling as though I had it all worked out and that Lucas was missing what was right in front of him.

"Sebastian I know it seems like a good idea at the moment but think about Jonas. Think about how he reacted to the thought of oversleeping," said Lucas gently.

"It was a bit much now that you mention it," understanding was dawning on me. Lucas said Jonas was a bit of an overreactor. He was already skittish with a threat from VI-Count.

"I don't think he can handle much more as it is," Lucas said.

"I agree but what about Rick?" I questioned.

"Rick is like a father figure to Jonas. I don't think he would be able to keep such a heavy load of information from Jonas. Plus Rick is a man who thinks he has been free from the cruel overlords like the Corp. He may seem strong but telling him about VI-Count might just cripple him. Sometimes we hold onto ideas or realities that we need to believe so that we can survive. If someone tries to take that away from us it could lead to disaster. Even someone who seems as strong as Rick" explained Lucas gently.

I said a temporary see you later to Lucas knowing that we would meet up again shortly. I headed to my quarters and decided to get cleaned up from the day will a shower. I was deep in thought and reflecting on all the day's events trying to the best of my ability to keep up with the continuing changing tide of viewpoint and information. I'm starting to see that I am severely limited in my ability to see who I can trust and who not to burden with the truth. I am so glad I am not in Lucas's shoes. It is hard enough to be in my shoes.

I wonder how Dimitri, Maddy, and Tyler are doing. I wonder if they received any new assignments. I was eager to catch up with Shawna as well. I haven't been able to fill her in about Aki, or the threat that Jonas received from VI-Count. I was so caught up in my head that the shower alarm was sounding shocking me back to the present. Two minutes go by way too quickly. It isn't fair. Why couldn't we have a five minute shower once a month. Would that truly be so bad? I mean if VI-Count is planning on bringing 95 more people into the Dome how is it that they can have a two minute shower as well? That proves there's enough water for everyone. Frustration was over taking me again. I just didn't understand why we were being treated so unfairly and being lied to over and over again. How limited where we really. I quickly got dressed in my only option for clothes and headed to the center. Eager for my answers.

Chapter 25

I wasn't in a hurry for dinner this evening. It was plain potato soup with potato bread. If they could find a way to make butter out of potatoes they would. Coming out of the Lower class quarters into the South wing with its low gray walls I entered what we called the Center. It was open and filled with light. It took a moment for my eyes to adjust. I headed to my favorite spot under the bridge located in the Center of the Dome. It was the closest thing to experiencing what life was like on earth before all the greedy corporations and human carelessness had completely destroyed any hope of anyone being able to enjoy the earth the way it should e enjoyed. If only people had appreciation and care then maybe we wouldn't be in this situation now. If people like VI-Count and Lord Baron or the Corp never existed. It was just wishful thinking and it was pointless.

It was too late. Never would I be able to enjoy what others took for granted. A seemingly simple act of walking through a forest of trees inhaling fresh pure air. Enjoying the energy released from all the life around. The smells of nature the sounds of different creatures scurrying around. I allowed myself to get lost in the possibilities. The sights, sounds and smells. Well to the best of what my imagination could come up with since I had never actually been able to experience these things. I am sure I was no were near to the real thing but it felt good to imagine. It was nice to have a moment of peace next to the little stream, it always had a calming effect on me.

I let my shoulders relax and tried to forget Jonas's distress. The look of fatigue and fear in his pale green eyes still seemed to hurt me a little. It was hard to see a grown man in such a state. So different from Rick one who had been hardened by the Corp. or even different from Lucas who's bright blue eyes were so full of what looked like courage in life despite his task. How could his eyes be so full of life was such a heavy load. I hoped I could be a bit like Lucas.
I kept trying to understand but I am struggling to make heads or tails of it. From a distance I saw Kelly and Aki walking along the trail. Which disturbed my recently acquired calm

state. Even the perfectly manicured green grass and flowering bushes off to the side could not bring it back. I did not like what I was seeing at all! This caught me off guard because I know Kelly really does not like him.

Yet she looked to be a bit dressed up. Her hair was done in away I had never seen it before and she even had on a pair of silver earrings they were shimmering against her dark complexion as the sun was slowly lying down to rest for the evening. As for the rest of the wardrobe she still had the standard gray on gray. But she brightened it with a light blue and gray scarf that set her eyes off. I love to look at her eyes which were blue as the ocean. They were my mother's eyes yet not.

Even Aki looked extra cleaned up. Having a uniform without any burn holes from his many hours of welding. His caramel complexion paled next to Kelly. He was a bit taller than Kelly a good 6 inches taller causing her to have to look up at him. Where Kelly had jet black curly hair Aki was bald with his head polished to a shine almost blinding me when the sun bounced off of it. They were engrossed in a deep conversation.

213

I peered over at Lucas through the bushes. He was over by the Ping Pong table with the others. Probably catching them up on the days events and seeing if they had anything to report. Although looking over at them you wouldn't know it. Tyler, Dimitri, Maddy, and Shawna all seemed to be laughing and enjoying themselves. The Center did have this effect on people. The openness I think helped to remove some of the weight off of our shoulders. Even if the lightened mood I could see the daggers Lucas was shooting out of his eyes towards Aki.

Even the Center could not have the desired effect on Lucas because of what he was taking in. If I was Aki I would drop the good guy act and run for my life. Aki and Kelly were only a few feet away so I stayed as still as possible while they approached and paused over top of the rustic wooden bridge. I could faintly hear their conversation over top of a gentle flow with a stream as the boards groaned over head from their weight.

"Thanks, Kelly for agreeing to walk with me this evening," Aki said so softly.

I am sure he was trying to gaze deeply into her eyes hoping to be romantic. This guy was a creep. I wanted to jump out and yell at Kelly telling her to get away. But that would draw a lot of attention. Although I didn't think that Lucas would mind all that much.

"No problem. I always enjoy walking around the track of the Dome at this time of day. It's so beautiful. The sun is gorgeous as it setting " Kelly said lacking the feeling that I think Aki was hoping for.

I could tell by the direction of her voice that she was looking out at the sunset as she spoke. I thought to myself good for her. Don't look at him I shouted in my head. He is so evil he might have some kind of mind control if you look into his lifeless brown eyes.

"Absolutely gorgeous," Aki sighed.

I got the impression he wasn't referring to the sunset.

"How was work today?" Kelly said quickly changing the subject.

I think she caught onto his meaning as well.

"It was work. Did some grinding and some weld repair on the North wing. General maintenance and upkeep. Painters will come tomorrow to seal the middle so that it will not rust over. How about you?" Aki asked with a slight tone of frustration accidentally seeping through his voice.

"Typical day as a crane operator," Kelly said passively.

"No more troubles?" Aki asked concerned.

"Nope, she seems to be good as new," Kelly said proudly.

"She? Since when is a crane considered to be a she?" Aki questioned.

"Since always," snapped Kelly.

"OK OK, I get it! The crane is a she, I will not argue with that. Kelly, I wanted to ask you something," Aki blurted out.

He seemed almost desperate. Like he knew his chance to ask was fading quickly.

"Do you think someone was behind or is behind the repairs that the Dome has had to undergo?" Aki asked quickly as if he feared not getting it out quick enough would mean he would never be free from this burden.

"What makes you say that?" Kelly said with a little surprise in her voice.

"I know repairs are normal and to be expected to some degree but what I've seen lately is far beyond normal. I feel like there's someone behind is Kelly. I want to find out who it is. They are interfering with VI-Count and all that he is doing to protect us. Can't you see that Kelly?" Aki asked with deep concern and belief in what he was saying.

I can tell by his tone that he wants Kelly to believe what he is saying as well, almost like he needs her to support him on this.

"I do agree that there are a lot more repairs. But you have to look at the big picture. We are running these machines 10 to 12 hours a day six days a week. We have been doing this for months now. That's more than normal use so we can expect repairs to be higher than normal," Kelly said with such confidence that I almost believed her even though I knew the truth!

She is good. Even when I think I couldn't care for Kelly anymore than I do she goes and makes me love her so much more!

"I guess you have a point but I still feel like there is something funny going on. Lord Byron has approached me," Aki said lowering his voice even more.

"He has? Does he feel the way you do?" Kelly asked calmly.

"Yes, but even more so. He asked me to look out for anything suspicious," Aki said.

"Does he have anyone in mind," Kelly asked.

"Yes, but I cannot say. I was told not to share this information with anyone I hope you understand it's nothing personal," Aki said pained that he could not share the information.

Kelly began "Oh, I guess that means since…"

Aki cut Kelly off mid-sentence. "Kelly, you know how I feel about you. I really care for you and your safety. I wish you would give me a chance. I could protect you and more than that I could also make you happy," Aki spoke as if a dam had burst inside of him, and now there was no way of turning back.

"Aki, we have talked about this. I respect you and I appreciate you and your feelings in your openness. But I do not want a relationship at this time," Kelly said firmly.

"Just because someone broke your heart 13 years ago Kelly. That's no reason to punish others.

You should allow yourself another chance. Look how much fun we had this evening. We could share many more evenings like this. Please you do not have to tell me your response now. Just promise me you'll think about it. I mean really think about it. I can promise you I will never abandon you. I will support you, care for you, and protect you each and every day," Aki vowed.

"Ok, I will think about it, I promise. And thank you for this evening, it was nice," Kelly said sincerely.

"That's all I ask. Thank you, Kelly," Aki said.

Yuck! This conversation is making my stomach hurt! Why in the world is Kelly agreeing to think about a proposal from the enemy! Aki is a traitor! How could she? It takes all I have not to speak. I start to taste blood. I realize that I was literally biting down on my tongue. My legs are cramping from swatting down behind the bushes for so long. Then just when I think the situation can I get any worse I hear Aki speak again.

"I know Lord Byron doesn't want me to share what he told me with anyone. But I do not want to keep anything from you Kelly. He told me to keep an eye out for Lucas," Aki said gravely.

"Lucas... Why Lucas?" Kelly asked trying to give her feelings away.

"Lord Byron has proof. I am not sure how. But he has proof that Lucas is connected with the outsiders. I wanted to warn you. Lucas is toxic. I am not sure if he has been trying to fill your mind and heart with poison but be sure he's trying to turn people against VI-Count! Be cautious. He is a dangerous man. You cannot trust him," Aki said.

"Thank you, Aki. I appreciate the warning. And thank you for caring enough to tell me I really appreciate it," said Kelly in a more matter-of-fact tone. She appreciates it! Aki is the toxic and poisonous one, not Lucas! What is she doing? I feel so betrayed, I feel like she's betraying her

self as well as Lucas keeping company with someone like him. I was about to blow it when the dinner bell rang. Aki and Kelly turned off the bridge heading towards the dining area. I laid-back flat on my back allowing my legs to once again have a flow of blood. As my legs tingled and

regained circulation Shawna plopped down beside me with a soft thud.

"That bad Huh?" Shawna asked with a half smile.

"Worse," I say flatly.

Quickly I filled her in. She was as disgusted and confused as I was. Her face became grim with concern.

"What are you gonna do?" she asked eagerly.

"I am going to confront Kelly," I said determined!

"Oh" was all that Shawna managed to say. By her face, I could tell she didn't think that was necessarily the wisest course.

Chapter 26

It took me 10 minutes to fill Shawna in on the note I found in the concrete mixer as well as the conversation I over heard. I also told her about Jonas. She felt so bad for Jonas. I could see the sadness in her eyes as I was recounting the day. Everyone was finishing up dinner. It didn't take too long to drink down the even more watery than usual potato soup. I grabbed a couple rolls and was about to speak up but Shawna told me to wait until after dinner. I let out an audible sigh. I was rewarded for this with a sharp look from Shawna.

"Not in front of the others," she hissed.

"Ok OK," I retorted.

After we finished I asked to speak to Kelly privately. She followed me over to a large area located behind the lounge area and ping-pong table. I made sure that we would be out of earshot of Dimitri and Tyler who were in the middle
of the game. Tyler really wasn't into playing ping pong but he was extremely competitive so he did

it for some bragging rights. Unfortunately, that didn't work out for him very well because Dimitri was demolishing him at this point. As was the case most times. So there wasn't gonna be any bragging on Tyler's end. You had to give it to Tyler for never giving up though. He was persistent he had that going for him.
Kelly could tell I was upset and she broke the silence first. Which I was grateful for, I honestly did not know how to start.

"Something on your mind?" she asked almost cautiously as if she already knew what was on my mind.

"How about you being on cahoots with the enemy? You're a traitor even worse than VI-Count!" I spit out the words like they are hot coals burning my tongue, knowing I won't get relief until they're off. My face grew hot with anger, borderline rage.

"Sebastian, don't talk to Kelly like that," Lucas defended, his tone coming off a bit stronger than I think he intended. I could see his protective nature coming out. I liked that about him normally but not now, he had to know!

"Don't defend her! You have no idea what she's done!" I said angrily.

I could feel the hot rage bubbling up, I felt like I was going to explode in frustration! I think Lucas was beginning to see that was something seriously wrong here. Finally!

"Kelly?' Lucas whispered sheepishly concerned, almost like he was afraid of what was to come. I know that he was keeping an eye on Kelly and Aki during their evening stroll, but he didn't hear the words. I bet if he did he wouldn't be so calm, and he definitely would not be defending her.

"It's not what you think, either of you," Kelly said, trying to soothe and cool the mounting blaze that was heading in her direction.

I could tell see was really fighting to keep her composure. How could she?

"I heard you! I heard you and Aki! I was under the Bridge the whole time," I charged.

"Sebastian look it's not what you think," Kelly repeated. If she said that phrase again I knew I was going to scream!

"It sure didn't look too much like nothing from where I was standing either," Lucas added scornfully. His cheeks grew red. Finally, he was speaking up!

"Grow up! The both of you! Aki likes me, everyone knows that. I don't return that affection everyone I thought knew that as well. I knew the only way to get him off my back even for a moment was if he thought that I would think about it," said Kelly firmly.

"Think about what exactly?" Lucas interrupted.

His face grew redder still.

"You know what Lucas, don't act stupid," Kelly snapped no longer about to keep her composure.

This interrogation was more than she cared for.

"Tell Lucas about what Aki said about Lord Byron," I said.

Refusing to hold anything back.

"What about Lord Byron?" Lucas asked with growing concern.

His face shifted to one more of concern and fear than anger.

"Lord Byron told Aki to keep an eye on you. He said that Lord Byron has proof of some kind that you were working with the outsiders. Lucas, you're in danger. I knew that Aki would only share this information with me if he thought he had a chance, I did this for the safety of everyone involved," Kelly said looking hurt that Lucas or I would ever think anything different.

Lucas and I sat silent, both feeling a bit ashamed. We both knew Kelly was smart. We both knew she did not like Aki. I know even if Lucas didn't that Kelly would still want to help protect me and maybe even him. Although she wouldn't admit that part.

"Sorry," I whispered embarrassed. Feeling deflated.

"It's OK," she said then gave me a hug.

This made me feel even smaller. I should have never doubted her, I know better than not to trust Kelly. All this deceit and deception is twisting me around in circles.

"We're all under a lot of pressure. It's hard to think clearly when there is so much going on." Kelly soothed.

Frustration from the moments before completely removed from her gentle, kind face. She always knows exactly what to say.

"I'm sorry Kelly," Lucas said heartily, not fully making eye contact with Kelly.

"You should be! You were acting like a fool," Kelly said sharply.

If it was not for her dark complexion I think her face would have topped Lucas's reddened face from earlier in the conversation.

"Jealousy does ugly things to people," Lucas said sheepishly.

Still unable to make eye contact.

"You have nothing to be jealous over. Move on, I have," Kelly said.

Lucas seemed crushed by her statement. It must have been hard for Lucas. Here Kelly forgave me so readily, yet she still could not would not forgive him. This was the second time in one day the my perspective had shifted reality. I really wanted to be on guard against that. Like with Lucas and his emotions. How they removed any semblance of clarity making it impossible to be rational or to see clearly. Even Kelly who continued to hold a grudge completely unwilling to see her part. I couldn't wait to fill Shawna in on the latest developments.

No sooner than the thought of Shawna

came into my head, she was there. How did she always do that. She seemed to know when I needed her the most. She had bounced over excitedly telling me that she had beat not only Tyler in ping-pong but also Dimitri. She was in such a good mood that her brown eyes seemed to have a sparkle. Her typical feisty attitude totally swallowed up by her glorious victory . And not a small one at that. She beat Tyler 15 to 1 and Dimitri 12 to 3. She was a little blinding Sun that was trying to force apart the gray storm clouds but I didn't even think she was aware of the mess she had just walked into. Maybe we were in the eye of it… My heart hurt at the thought of taking that joy away from her and handing her the darkness. I just couldn't do it to her. I was interrupted by my internal debate by the attention Shawna was giving to Kelly. I thought that maybe she could see the pain in Kelly's face. Shawna was gazing at not Kelly exactly, but instead at her earrings. Shawna then broke the silence.

"Those earrings are so beautiful Kelly. I've never seen you wear earrings before. Are they new?" Shawna asked curiously.

228

This was an odd question because Shawna knew that Kelly could not just go out and buy earrings. Stores didn't exist and they hadn't for over 12 years. The Dome sure didn't have a store. Maybe she was caught up in the moment and wasn't thinking clearly. Or maybe it was a crafty way to get information without seeming to be too nosy.

"No, they are not new. I've had them for quite some time. I don't remember where they came from exactly," Kelly said although it wasn't convincing.

If I didn't know better I would think that it was an outright lie.

"You don't remember! Wow! That's hurtful," Lucas said offended.

The red flush returned to his face yet again.

"Do you mean to say you got them for her Lucas?" Shawna asked a bit surprised by the development.

I did not picture Shawna as the romantic type but she really seemed to enjoy this revelation.

"Why yes I did. Don't sound so shocked. It was our third date. I took Kelly to Lillys Point

229

Lookout. It was one of my favorite spots and I wanted to share it with one of my favorite people. It was high above the valley. You can look for miles. And the sunset was beautiful. More beautiful than any sunset ever viewed from the Dome," Lucas said a bit coldly at the end.

Jealousy was obviously still clouding his judgment.

"I didn't think you were romantic type. Go, Lucas!" Shawna said with a grin.

Really drinking up this story. This made Lucas smile warmly at Shawna, I think it made him feel good that someone was appreciating the effort he went through.

"I picked out that spot and those earrings for a reason. The two stars interlocked were to represent Kelly and I. Nothing was ever to tear us apart. I thought being so close to the stars with our location would've been a nice touch," Lucas said proudly.

It almost seemed as though he was no longer here with us but instead back to that moment in time when all was right between him and Kelly. A sadness that he tried to conceal clouded his face for a brief moment as he was shifted back into the present.

"That's deep Lucas," I said amazed and meant it.

I was learning more and more about Lucas. He was a complex man. There was much more to him than I ever thought possible. I was also wondering how Kelly could still hold this grudge against a man who clearly still loved her very deeply.

"Go on go on," Shawna repeated eagerly.

She looked like a little schoolgirl not wanting to miss a single detail.

"I even packed a dinner picnic. We had warm roast and green beans," Lucas was trying to finish the menu but Kelly jumped in and cut him off.

"No, we had warm ham, macaroni, and cheese with Caesar salad. You know I don't like roast. You even had brownies for dessert my favorite with a star on top with icing," Kelly corrected.

Then blushed went she realized Lucas's deceit. Shawna and I looked at each other and smiled. Lucas had just tricked Kelly into admitting that she remembered not only where the earrings came from but also the night that he gave them to her. Man Lucas is good! I need to remember that play in case I ever needed it later. Lucas and Kelly just stood there for a long moment stunned. I think Lucas was touched by Kelly remembering in such detail the night of so long ago. Why had she told us she didn't remember it when she clearly did? Adults, I really don't think I will understand them ever. I wonder what happens to one's brain when they go from you know smart children to a totally different way of reasoning and seeing things. I wonder if it would be possible to prevent that part from happening to me. I would like to keep my reasoning for sure. Adults like I said are a bit strange sometimes and they don't seem to have the ability to see it.

"So you do remember that night 14 years ago!" Lucas said with a sly grin.

Making a face I think he was hoping looked debonair but honestly, I think he might have been a bit out of practice because Shawna and even Kelly let out a small chuckle. Lucas didn't blush or seem to mind which led me to believe he made that botched debonair face on purpose. Man, he is so good!

"14 years ago! Yikes! You two must be old! Since I was only two years old then!" Shawna said jokingly.

"Ha ha! Very funny," Kelly said with a smile.

The dark mood in the air had shifted. The clouds were parting and now the storm had cleared. I'm so glad that Shawna came over. Like I said a little bright piece of sunshine. She even brought out Lucas's even more playful side with was fun to see. Even Kelly was in a bit better place.

"That was the night I realized I wanted to spend the rest of my life with Kelly. The very next date I asked her to marry me," Lucas said proudly as he recalled the memory.

Then as if ripped out of a perfect dream the reality of the situation can crashing down around us. I was right, we were only in the eye of the storm. Now it began to rage once more. I do not even think Shawna could save us now. A shade of gray and even a bit of thunder seemed to fill the room. We could feel the electric between Lucas and Kelly. It was not pleasant.

"Anyway, that was a long time ago ancient history!" Kelly blurted suddenly.

Her calm and gentle face turning into a scowl.

"Must not be too ancient because you're still wearing my earrings!" Lucas said.

Not trying to hide his hurt any longer. I think that they forgot we were there for a brief moment.

"They are not your earrings they are my earrings. If I could remove your star without harming the other I would!" Kelly said angrily.

"It would have been less painful if you would have just let them stay together," Lucas whispered faintly.

He looked so wounded. His shoulders slumped and the light in his blue eyes faded like life have been sucked out of them. Even his light peachy complexion had lost life and turned pale. He was biting the lower left side of his lip again. I could tell he was deep in thought after a few moments all that he said was,

"How many times do I have to tell you that I am sorry? How long are you going to remain blinded to your part, even after all that you have learned?"

With that, he simply turned and walked away. Even with Kelly's dark brown complexion, I could see her cheeks turn red and her eyes fill with tears from hurt and I imagined a bit of embarrassment too. She stood there stunned. Her short stature looked almost childlike. No longer did Her ocean-like blue eyes have energy. The wind was no longer blowing over but was now still, sad and silent. Shawna and I did not say a word. We just uncomfortably remained. Unsure of what to do or what to say. I felt as if we left Kelly at that moment she may have crumbled under Lucas's words. We all knew, even Kelly that Lucas was right. All Lucas ever wanted to do was protect, love, and care for her. But she was so wrapped up in VI-Count's lies, she chose to trust the wrong man. I could now see some tears falling from the corner of Kelly's eyes down her dark cheeks. Like lonely rivers without an end.

"He's got a point you know. He would have done anything for me. But I couldn't do one thing for him. I couldn't trust him like he wanted, like he needed, like he deserved. He saw right through

VI-Count. While I was so blinded with fear that I pushed him away. I pushed Lucas away," Kelly merely whispered the last part. Her shoulders even more slumped than Lucas's.

Then like Lucas, she should turned and walked away. I was going to follow after her but Shawna grabbed my shoulder. I instantly covered my head for fear of a wall once again making contact or something equally as hard. This was a typical occurrence when Shawna put her hand on my shoulder. I felt foolish when I opened my eyes because there were no walls closer than 15 feet. But I couldn't be too careful where Shawna was involved.

"Let her go. There is nothing you can say or do to ease her pain right now," Shawna said mournfully. Her eyes pleading with me.

Chapter 27

"I feel so bad for the both of them. They both were doing what they felt was right," I said reflecting on all that I had just taken in.

"That's the thing though they couldn't both be right. Someone had to be wrong. And Kelly knows that now it was never Lucas, but it was her. It's a heavy burden she has just discovered," Shawna said.

I could see all of this had hit her pretty hard. For two people who really cared for each other so deeply, then to be torn apart from within.

"Poor Lucas, poor Kelly. There is something else that has probably hit Kelly really hard as well adding to the weight of this situation," I said, my heart broken for them both.

"What is that?" Shawn nudged gently.

"Kelly blamed my mom all these years for what she thought was abandonment. Realize that my mom was right to some degree must be flooding over her as well," I said grimly.

"Oh man, this is crazy. Kelly's whole world has just been flipped upset down. All the misdirected anger and hurt. I am sure now she's not really sure what to do with it all. This is gonna take sometime for her to work through," Shawna said somberly.

"Man do you think VI-Count can really fathom all the damage that he is done? He has to know, I know he does. It's just so hard to wrap your mind around the reality that someone could be so cruel and truly evil. To not care about anyone at all but his own selfish interest," I said feeling so frustrated unsure what to make of all of this.

"It's unnatural that is for sure. We have to be careful Sebastian we can not limit what VI-Count is willing to do to get his way, or what he will do to those…" Shawna trailed off not even wanting to finish the thought out loud.

With that thought we soberly and somberly walked back to the South wing to go back to our quarters for the evening. The narrow gray corridor seemed even more narrow constricting even. I was so exhausted that I just nodded to Shawna as she reached her quarters first. Being equally tired she didn't speak but turned and entered her quarters I felt as though I was going to fall asleep walking. I finally made it to my small sorry excuse for living quarters. When my head hit the sorry excuse for a pillow and my body felt the sleep-stealing sheets I didn't think my fatigue would be able to conquer such discomfort even in my exhausted state. I was so physically and emotionally drained from the day that I thought even their efforts would be futile.

Jonas, Rick, Lucas, Kelly the other teens, their lives were playing out before me. There were so many lives that VI-Count and the Corp. hurt and destroyed and even ended. What was gonna happen next? How were we going to get out from under the powerful and cruel hand of VI-Count? How were we going to do this before the Corp entered the Dome? I was unsure of so much even my ability to decipher reality and truth. So much of what I thought I knew was in fact a lie. With these thoughts, I drifted into a restless sleep.

Chapter 28

I woke up with a bit of a start. I had finally fallen asleep but I felt like I had only been out for a matter of minutes. I still felt a bit hung over from the intense emotions of the evening before. As I was getting the cobwebs out of my brain something came to me I never thought of before. Shawna and I had stumbled over the truth about the vitamins and the shots that we were given by Maxine and Logan.

Tyler, Maddy, and Dimitri are so clearheaded about it all. How was it that they avoided the vitamins and the boosters shots? How did they initially find out the truth about the vitamins and shots? I don't know how I would've felt if someone came to me with this kind of information if I was still foggy-headed from the medication I was given.

I made a mental note to ask them about that a little later in the day. As I was standing up and getting myself together there was an urgent banging on my door.

"Sebastian get up!" Shawna yelled through the door.

Her voice was a bit muffled but I recognized her voice right away. I also recognized the urgency in her voice and knew that it was something serious. I hurried to the door and as I pulled it open Shawna pushed her way in knocking me back causing me to hit my head on the wall once again.

"OUCH!" I cried out in pain. "You have to stop doing that! You are going to give me another concussion," I spat irritated.

"No time for that," Shawna said frantically.

"No time for me to rub my head after you yet again bashed my head against the wall. I'm starting to think that you do this on purpose." I said exasperated.

"Will you stop your blubbering and listen to me!" Shawna shouted.

By her face, I could see that it was indeed serious.

"I am listening to you but you haven't said anything except no time for that. No time for what? What is going on?" I said impatiently.

"Kelly has been kidnapped!" Shawna exclaimed.

"What? How do you know?" I asked confused.

Maddy came running into the room interrupting Shawna's explanation.

"Shawna, Sebastian I found this in the hallway right outside of Kelly's room," Maddy said holding up an earring.

But not just any earring, the very earring we had just seen Kelly wearing last night. Two stars interlocked. We had just heard the story and everything. Knowing how much it meant to her. Yet here the earring is in Maddy's hands, with not Kelly to be seen. My heart sank. Panic wanted to overtake me, I needed to know what was going on!

"Will someone please tell me what in the world is happening?" I shouted.

That seemed to get everyone's attention, finally!

"Around 5 o'clock this morning, I heard scuffling in Kelly's room. I went to investigate but Kelly was missing. Her door was left wide open and she was nowhere to be found in the room. I looked down the corridor and a couple of feet away from the doorway was this earring." Maddy explained.

"I heard it as well but like Maddy, I was too late," Shawna said seeming to be disappointed in herself for allowing this to happen to Kelly, like it was her responsibility to protect everyone.

"Lucas, we have to tell him, he'll know what to do," I said confidently.

At that, all three of us raced down the hall to Lucas's room. We started banging on the door frantic hoping that he hadn't left for work yet.

"I'm coming, I'm coming! Cool your horses!" Lucas slowly came to the door taking his sweet time completely unaware of the news we were about to share.

Couldn't he hear the panic in our banging?

"Come on, come on" I repeated to myself impatiently.

"Good morning to you too…" He stopped mid-sentence when he saw the three of us standing there in front of his door faces full of fear.

"Kelly's missing!" Maddy blurted out.

"What do you mean she is missing? Lucas snapped, his light complexion turning red with concern.

"Maddy and I heard scuffling in Kelly's room this morning we rushed over but it was too late! The only thing we found was this ear ring in the hallway a few feet from her door," Shawna managed to explain.

Lucas did not have to ask about the ear ring he knew it was Kelly's since he was the one who had given it to her all those years ago. He held it close to his heart as he tried to assess the The situation in his mind as quickly as possible. I knew he was mulling over the situation because he was biting on his lower lip again. This showed that he was deep in thought trying to put pieces in the place. I felt like I must've been missing half of the puzzle so I wasn't sure how in the
world we were going to figure this out. After a few moments, Lucas finally spoke up.

"Yesterday was a trick!" Lucas exclaimed.

So irritated at himself for not seeing it. He was so busy being angry at Kelly that he totally missed what was really going on right before his eyes.

"Idiot," Lucas muttered to himself.

"Aki knows how you feel about Kelly, everyone does. That was an act, wasn't it?" Shawna asked catching on more quickly than I was.

"Yes and it's gonna work too because Aki and Lord Byron know that I will not let anything happen to Kelly!" declared Lucas.

Before any of us could say anything Lucas was off racing down the hall on his way to find Aki. What could we do? He was willingly running right into a trap! My mind is spinning thinking about the amount of effort that Aki and Lord Byron put into this plan. It made my blood boil to think about what they may be doing to Kelly. I knew that I had to do something to help but I wasn't sure what. I felt like my hands were tied.

Chapter 29

"I have to go after them I can't let anything happen to Kelly!" I said determined to protect my aunt from Aki in Lord Byron.

"I'm going with you!" said Shawna.

I already knew she wouldn't let me go alone. There was no point in arguing with her.

"Me too!" Maddy chimed.

Which caught me off guard. I thought Maddy was a nice person but I didn't really know her that well. We had been forced together as of late but other than the past few days I didn't know anything about her. I was touched that she wanted to help but I was still unsure. As I was trying to work out in my brain what to do Shawna's voice broke through.

"We need all the help that we can get Sebastian," Shawna said firmly.

Again I knew better than to argue.

"All right it's settled let's go," I said only I wasn't sure which way to go. Maddy seemed to pick up on my hesitation.

"This way! I think Aki probably took Kelly through the back tunnel," Maddy said pretty confidently.

"What's the back tunnel?" Shawna and I asked in unison.

"The back tunnel as a hidden corridor located at the end of the South wing that takes you to an underground bunker," Maddy explained.

"Why would Aki take Kelly there?" I asked confused.

"There is a secret exit from the bunker to the outside," Maddy said.

"Secret, hidden, creepy dirt tunnels, evil rulers, this place just keeps getting better and better," Shawna said sarcastically.

"The hidden bunker was for the Lower class in case of an emergency situation supposedly. Although I imagine that was a lie too. Vl-Count and the Nobles don't really care about our safety as you know. It was probably a lie to get us to build it in the first place. Well not us seeing that I was only two when it was built," Maddy said matter-of-factly.

"How do you know about it then?" Shawna asked before I could.

"Lucas," was all Maddy said.

Her face suddenly filled with great sadness. Realization dawned on me. Her concern and care were for Lucas. He had been her protector as well as parent for these last 12 years. Not just to her but to Tyler and Dimitri as well. That is why she is so eager to help. Lucas means just as much to her as Kelly means to me. Even more so because my parents are still alive while Maddy isn't so sure about hers. As we were headed towards the tunnel Tyler jogged up beside us. His hair looking ruffled more than usual and his cool demeanor was replaced with a frantic one. Even though Tyler was sporty and in pretty good shape he seemed to be huffing and puffing.

"Maddy where is Lucas we got bad news, I need to talk to him right away," Tyler spoke quickly between breaths we almost weren't able to make out what he said.

"Not right now Tyler. We don't have time," Maddy said dismissively.

"You have to! VI-Count has called for an outing to get supplies," Tyler said gravely.

"What?" Maddy smacked her forehead "Not now, of all times why does it have to be now?"

"Why would VI-Count want us to go out to gather supplies and why now? He has never asked us to do anything like this before. He has always told us that the outside air was poisonous and then we would not be able to survive." Shawna spoke out loud more to herself than to any of us.

She seemed to be trying to put a puzzle together that was missing pieces and mixed up with another puzzle that didn't belong. I could see her light brown eyes darting side to side as if she was running out of time, and she knew it.

"Shawna's right, VI-Count has never asked us to go outside to get supplies before. So what is this really about ?" I asked our group.

"I think VI-Count is trying to ensure that the Lower class are out-of-the-way," Tyler said confidently. Realization suddenly dawned on me. I reflected back to the conversation that Lucas had with me.

"VI-Count is bringing in the Corp," I said.

"This was all part of a trap. Unfortunately, Lucas took the bait. Aki and Lord Barron played him. They knew that he would not let anything happen to Kelly. Now that Lucas is gone it'll be easier for VI-Count to get rid of the Lower class," as I spoke Shawna's eyes grew wide with concern.

"Aki is luring them to the underground hideout, isn't he? The place where they intend to get rid of the Lower class members?" Shawna said with a measure of shock disbelief and understanding all tangled into one conglomerate of emotion and thinking.

"Lucas told us VI-Count's new plans. VI-Count and Lord Byron have rigged a cave," Tyler was explaining until Maddy cut him off.

"We know what's going to happen Tyler! But we're not helping anyone standing around here talking about it. We need to get moving. Lucas and Kelly are in grave danger, along with everyone else in the Dome. We're the only ones that know the truth. We need to do something and we need to do it now!" Maddy said motivating us all into action.

Her once bookworm demeanor was replaced with one of a warrior. With that, we all headed for the hidden corridor. From my experience with the tunnel that Shawn and I have used near the dining hall to the West Wing I was a little skeptical and nervous about what we were going to encounter. I was hoping it wouldn't be as inky black or as grungy as that tunnel. Not that I am scared of the dark or of a little dirt or anything. These are completely normal concerns.

Maddy stopped at the end of the South wing at what seemed to be a random location. There were no latches or door hinges. Maddy was simply running her hand along the gray wall until she found a seam. Halfway up the wall was a light mounted just above my head. There was a small recessed button behind the fixture Maddy explained. She simply pushed the button and a section of the wall opened up. It was like an old-fashioned pocket door where it slid right into itself. We passed through. As soon as we were through the door it shut behind us again. It was totally dark in the hidden room until Maddy turned on a flashlight. Maddy wore a utility belt at all times. She seemed to have something for every occasion on it. I was glad she came along. Maddy flipped the switch on her flashlight and light flooded the room. I exhaled. I didn't even realize that I had been holding my breath.

Apparently, I was not the only one, I heard a few other sighs around me. There really wasn't much to the tunnel. It looked a lot like our rooms just a bit narrower yet larger. It even had the same homey gray color that we were used to. Maddy quickly went to the West wall.

"Sebastian, Tyler, we need to slide this cabinet out of the way. The exit is hidden behind it." Maddy commanded with no trace of doubt in her voice, demonstrating her explicit trust in Lucas.

I was also overwhelmed by her trust in Tyler and me to be able to move that so-called cabinet. It was so large and bulky. It looked as if it was made with the Watchman's strength in mind. It was clear this exit was not for the Lower Class. I was beginning to see a side of Maddy that I didn't even know existed. When I looked at her I no longer saw a bookworm in her brown eyes that hid behind her purple glasses but I saw that warrior inside that had completely taken over earlier. The warrior that I was sure was not gonna leave until Lucas was safe. It has been reinforced in me yet again not to judge by outward appearances. Now they were filled with determination. She was no pushover she was a good leader and she was very commanding of our attention and obedience. This made it easier for us to trust her. Even under this stress, she was completely together. Her should length black hair flawlessly in place. Her glasses not askew but instead sitting perfectly on the bridge of her nose. Utility belt stripped tightly in place. You can tell she had trained for this. She was ready. And Tyler too. He was completely different. He wasn't full of complaints and arguments. He simply did what Maddy asked. His green eyes were filled with a similar determination as Maddy's. They both seemed to have the same driving force. Wanting to protect and save Lucas, as he had done for them all these years in the absence of their parents.

I was starting to feel a bit guilty. All that I had been thinking about was Kelly and her safety. Tyler and I were having a difficult time straining trying to get the cabinet out of the way so Maddy and Shawna quickly jumped in. Finally, we were able to push it aside. We all gasped not expecting to see an old-fashioned lock on the door.

"Where did anyone get one of those?" Tyler exclaimed.

"It's an ancient relic, how do you even unlock one? There's no handprint sensor, no thumbprint sensor, know eye scanner!" Shawna said dumbfounded.

"It takes what's called a key. Before biosensors, they had metal keys that had teeth on them to line up to release the mechanisms inside the lock. They're actually very easy to crack it shouldn't take me more than a couple of seconds," Maddy said confidently.

Maddy quickly got her tools together and got to work. She pulled a narrow black pick from her utility built. Why in the world did she have a lock pick? You know when you watch a movie or read a book and someone in the story just happens to have the right tool for the job matter what that tool or job may be. Well, that is Maddy. Within seconds she had to lock off the latch. We all eyeballed her in amazement.

"What?" Maddy exclaimed noticing that all eyes were on her.

"It was really no big deal, any of you could have done it," Maddy said defensively.

"No, no we could not have Maddy, you are amazing! Never doubt that!" Tyler said his face matching his words.

We all nodded in agreement. With that, we were off. I was starting to wonder if I would ever again be able to walk instead of run. I had been running on adrenaline for so long now I knew that I was going to crash and that my body was not able to continue at this pace. I was grateful that the cobwebs had been walked through already. Aki and Kelly along with Lucas must've looked like oversized Q-tips when they exited the tunnel. The walls were covered with what remained of the webs but the middle was clear. I just hope that the web has been vacant for some time now. Even the toughest of men can be brought down by a spider. So it was totally normal for me to scream at what I thought was a spider feeling down on the top of my head. Maddy and Shawna gave me a look.

"Grow up you big baby!" Shawna shot at me.

"It's just a piece of rust, it's not gonna hurt you," Maddy said mockingly joining in with Shawna.

"You guys wouldn't have been so calm if it had fallen on you. You're just as creeped out as I am. Stop acting like you're not!" I spat indignantly.

Irritated by the fact they both were ganging up on me even snickering. Tyler didn't say anything. I had a feeling he didn't like spiders or the dark either. His cocky demeanor was completely gone. Finally, after five minutes of running, we could see a glimmer of daylight at the end of the tunnel. Lucas did not even bother shutting the hatch tightly. I guess he was in much of a hurry to think about shutting the door behind him. Whatever the case we burst through without skipping a beat. We must've traveled a lot quicker since we were running and did not have a fighting hostage because, within a few minutes, we spotted Lucas hot on Aki and Kelly's trail.

"There they are!" shouted Tyler.

We ran at top speed. We were losing sight of them we had to keep up. They quickly disappeared behind a large rock face.

"We need to be as quiet as possible from this point on. We do not know what we might find on the other side," Maddy warned without a speck of fear.

We all ran as quickly and quietly as possible. When we finally reached the rock wall we
were all trying to quietly gasp for breath. We were not out of shape by any means. We did just run almost 5 miles in a very short period of time. We could breathe outside but it was difficult. Years and years of mismanagement of the earth have caused the oxygen levels to decrease. So this
was a lot of stress to our bodies. We were all feeling it. Once we got ourselves together we began to start our accent to get a better view. What we saw horrified us!

Chapter 30

Brutus, Danny, and Hank the Watchmen on the outside were standing in front of Lucas who was now sprawled out on the floor beaten and blooded. Danny had a black eye forming. Lucas must've got a hold of him before he was knocked down. Hank's knuckles were a bit blooded. Lucas must've really put up a fight I thought to myself. Kelly was handcuffed to the wall of the cave crying. Helpless. Rage filled in my throat and as I tried to swallow it down. My fingernails dug into my fist because they were bald so tight. Tyler, Maddy and Shawna looked equally as angry. It was so frustrating standing here watching knowing we could not do anything at this moment but watch. Our hands were tied, if we jumped in now we would be beaten and restrained as well, or even worse. That would not do anybody any good. I noticed Aki over to the side talking to Aaron. He was one of the Watchman from the inside of the Dome. We definitely knew we did not stand a chance against him. He was the largest of the Watchman.

He stood six foot three a solid wall of muscle. Jet black hair and steely lifeless gray eyes.

"That's the creep that found Quinn," Tyler spat, rage filling his face. His eyes were mere slights as he stared daggers at Aaron.

"Shush! You are going to get us all caught," Shawna hissed reminding us all to be quiet.

"There's Hank and Lord Byron," I whispered as quietly as possible so as not to get a look from Shawna or betray our position.

"What are they doing here," Shawna whispered back.

I shrugged, her guess was as good as mine.

"Look," Maddy pointed.

"Oh no," Shawna groaned.

My eyes followed her gaze. My heart sank to the floor when my eyes finally fell on what Shawna was referring to. There was a long fat black cable running along the wall. It ran right behind Kelly about level with her waist. It stretched the length of the entire cave. The cave itself was not all that big. We could see pretty much all of the walls. It was long and narrow, around 35 feet wide and 70 feet long. In the back of the cave, there were four large boxes. I couldn't make out what the labels said. Maddy quickly pulled out what looked like a tiny monocular. I was so grateful for Maddy and her utility belt that did not have an end!

"It says explosives," Maddy whispered in disbelief.

Realization hitting as VI-Count's plan was right here in front of us. He was really gonna do this. He was going to kill innocent people. The same people who had trusted him and his protection. Lord Byron's cold voice rang out to the cave. His face looked more sinister than ever. You could see that he was enjoying this. We all held our breath and listened.

"The rest of the Lower class will be here shortly. Be sure to cover the boxes. We don't want them to figure out what's going on beforehand. VI-Count and I along with you have waited for this moment for long enough. It's time to get rid of those rats. No longer will we have to live with their deplorable kind," Lord Byron said menacingly.

"You got it, boss," Aaron replied pleased immensely by Lord Byron's instructions.

"What about this one?" Brutus asked pointing to Lucas's limp body on the floor. His greased-back hair and cold black eyes looked even more frightening with a villainess grin that now erupted on his face. You can see that he wanted to finish Lucas himself.

"Leave that trader on the floor, in the dirt where he belongs!" Lord Byron commanded with satisfaction.

Brutus' look shifted from one of sheer joy to disdain.

"What if he wakes up?" Brutus asked almost in a pleading voice like one from a little boy who was denied a toy.

"He won't be waking up anytime soon the way Hank and Danny worked him over," Aaron reassured.

Brutus was still not satisfied but he knew better than to go on.

"Remember wait until all the Lower class members are in the cave. Repeat to them the instructions they received this morning. Give them a list of the supplies they are supposed to gather. Have their gear in the cave so they can spend some time gathering it. This will give you ample opportunity to get out before you detonate. Make sure none of the kids accidentally came along. We need those little rats to continue to build and maintain the Dome. Do not mess this up. If you do VI-Count will have your heads," Lord Byron said coldly.

The Watchman did not question further. Even with their size, they did not dare go against Lord Byron or VI-Count. They knew firsthand what VI-Count was capable of.

"What? They are gonna use us to do all the work?" Tyler said in shock.

This apparently was a new development that Lucas had not warned any of us about. I could see his reason for holding back. It definitely would have made it more difficult to keep our heads clear for the mission. I could see a shift in Tyler already within seconds of learning the plan. His typical cool laid-back demeanor was completely erased and replaced with one of fear and dread.

" VI-Count and the Corp will probably try to work us to death, we have to do something," Maddy said matter of factly.

Not allowing the warrior to slip. I was grateful. If we were all handling the news like Tyler we would be doomed for failure.

"Don't worry, we have everything covered," Hank reassured Lord Byron.

"What about the other traders Maya, Malcolm, Stella, and their leader Emmett?" Asked the smaller and not as bright Watchman Danny.

Aaron and Brutus just cut him a look that made him stop talking. They seemed almost embarrassed by Danny and his stupidity.

"They won't be a problem. Brutus has already taken care of them. They're tied up and hidden further back in the cave. They are no longer a threat. Their little uprising has caused their very downfall," Lord Byron said proudly.

His grey eyes filled with pride because of his triumph.

"I have heard their names before, Lucas has spoken of them," Maddy whispered.

"Malcolm and Maya are my parents," said Shawna meekly.

I see fear and concern on her face. I understood why. To come so far to wait so long to see them. And now faced with the news that we might just lose them forever. The situation felt so bleak and so hopeless. It was driving me nuts not being able to do anything but just sit back and watch all this happen. There was no way that we could stand up against Brutus, Hank, or Aaron. VI-Count had planned everything so perfectly. I was pulled out of my thoughts by Maddy's question.

"Who are Emmett and Stella? I mean I know that Emmett is the leader of the outside, but are they your parents Sebastian," Maddy asked as if she was almost afraid to ask.

A sadness filled her brown eyes, one that was so deep her glasses could not hide.

"Yes, Emmett and Stella are my parents," I said softly afraid if I said it too loudly Maddy might lose her warrior and crumble before my very eyes.

I did not want that, I too would not be able to handle that. I felt like we were all so fragile in this moment. A mere breath would blow us all away.

"That confirms it doesn't it Maddy? Our parents are dead. I mean if they were alive wouldn't they be with Sebastian and Shawna's parents," Tyler spoke below a whisper, his voice barely
audible.

He knew the answer already you could tell by his eyes and his face. But it was as if he needed confirmation for Maddy before it to be true for him to be 100 percent sure.

Maddy didn't say anything she just nodded her head and looked down at her feet. She looks so broken so frail in that moment. The commanding warrior Maddy was gone. Replaced by a feeble shell. I think in her heart and in Tyler's heart they had hoped more than anything that their parents were alive somewhere and they would see them again.

But now they knew the truth. The one that Lucas never told them. He knows what it would've done to them. I never shared with them the truth either, I couldn't. It's just not fair! Maddy and Tyler both had tears streaming down their faces. Shawna and I cannot do anything but watch mournfully. Guilt weighed on my mind and heart so heavy now. Here me and Shawna have our parents mere feet away from us.

All this emotion was more than I could bear. Shawna and I joined Maddy and Tyler in their tears. All the frustrations of the day, the anxiety, the stress, the deceit, the reality that our entire lives in the Doom we were used, we were all used and lied to. The weight flooded over us in an instant of time. It felt like we sat there for an eternity.

We were startled by the sound of shifting feet. We all turned to look around to see Dimitri. He was squatted behind us. I can see in his deep brown eyes that he had heard our conversation. His black hair was matted down with sweat. And his face was soaked in tears. No one spoke for a while longer. The moment was broken by the sounds of Brutus, Danny, Aaron, and Hank finishing up and finally leaving the cave. It was only after Aaron gave Lucas one last kick to the ribs which was followed by a groan.

Chapter 31

"We need to do something before those goons come back!" Shawna demanded a fire under her that seemed to be inextinguishable.

It was just the energy and motivation we needed in that moment. My mind was racing. We needed to get out of here and we had to do it quickly. Everything was set up in the cave. The last element would be for the Lower class members to arrive. And they would do that at any moment. We had to move fast. Maddy was the first to act. It looked like the warrior was once again resurrected from the ashes. Without a word of warning, she simply jumped down from the cave floor. It was about a 6-foot drop. Kelly gasped in fright.

"Maddy, what are you doing here? It's not safe you need to leave before Brutus and the rest of the muscle comes back," Kelly said firmly with noticeable irritation in her voice.

Tyler, Dimitri, Shawn, and I followed Maddy's lead dropping to the floor. Kelly was stunned. She wasn't sure what to say. Her mouth kept twisting as if all her questions and demands were tangled up leaving no room for anything else to escape. Lucas let out a moan. Dimitri was by his side in an instant.

"Lucas, talk to me are you hurt," Dimitri pleaded, his deep brown eyes filled with tears.

"Of course, he's hurt dummy. He just got jumped by those brick walls. Don't you see the blood?" Tyler spat.

I was beginning to think that Tyler used his jerk persona as a protection, or wall of some kind. But it was hard to not want to punch him in the face for acting in this way. Can't he see that Dimitri is shaken up?

"Lucas! Please, talk to me," Dimitri said gently, ignoring Tyler.

Grateful that Dimitri had more patience with jerk faces than I did. Maddy joined them on the floor as I walked over to Kelly.

"Are you all right?" I asked gently.

"Mostly," Kelly said with heartache.

"I can't believe Aki is working with VI-Count. This was all the trap. I feel so stupid. This is all my fault. Poor Lucas, poor, poor Lucas," Kelly repeated with hurt then went deeper than my time on the earth.

Deeper than my ability to understand or comprehend. Even so, I had to offer some comfort, it broke my heart to see her like this. And the thought that she was blaming herself was wrong. This was not her fault. It was VI-Counts and VI-Counts alone. "It's not your fault Kelly, You are not stupid. No one is ever stupid for believing in and trusting people. The stupid ones are the ones who take advantage of people's kindness and compassion and turn their strengths into weapons." I said firmly.

I could see the guilt Kelly was feeling all over her face. It was painful for me to see her in such distress. My words at this time were not going through, and I could not accept them too. She had just gone through a very traumatic experience. It would take time for her to be able to process and work through this. I had to be patient and gentle. I had to keep my emotions and frustration in check.

"Poor Lucas. He ran right into this trap, even though he knew what was happening. Only if I hadn't been so stupid, so naïve," Kelly said.

She looks so ashamed so deflated like all the

wind has been knocked out of her. It was difficult because she also looked so unsure. Kelly was always someone with a plan she knew what was coming next.

"Can't blame yourself, Kelly. You're a good kind and compassionate person. I know it's hard to even imagine people being so cruel. You are not to blame. VI-Count and the other Noble's are! Not you," I said more firmly than I had intended.

I know it is gonna take time for her to see but I can not keep letting her repeat these lies, I do not want them to sound down into her heart and remain there. It was just too much for me to see her like this. I needed her to be strong. I need her not to internalize guilt that did not belong to her. It was not hers to take on. It was a fine speech but what now I thought to myself. How were we supposed to stop the Lower class members from entering into this trap? There was no way we could fight Brutus or any of the other Watchmen. They were solid muscle on top of solid muscle. It would break my hand if I were to punch Brutus in the face instead of breaking his jaw. Shawna called me over.

"Lucas is in really bad shape. I don't think he is going to be able to help. We are going to have to carry him out of here. How about Kelly? Can you get the straps off of her?" Shawn asked.

Straps! I smacked my forehead. Everyone was so busy and wrapped up in our conversations that we totally forgot to free Kelly!

"I'll do that now," I said then quickly ran over.

She was tied with simple ropes that I could easily cut through if I had a knife. But you don't generally need knives in the Dome so unfortunately I was fresh out. Then I remembered, Maddy! She has everything in her utility belt!

"Maddy, do you have a knife?" I asked hurriedly without looking down.

She reached into her utility bill and pulled out a little red block with rounded edges. On one of the sides it read "Swiss Army knife".

"What is a Swiss army and why do you have their knife?" I asked bewildered.

"It's only one of the greatest inventions of all time. I cannot believe you have never heard of a Swiss Army knife!" Maddy said with disdain.

"I can't know everything now, can I? I shot back defensively. This thing is an ancient relic just

271

like the lock on the door that you picked earlier," I spat frustration that I could not contain coming out.

I needed to get it together. Maddy did not deserve that. She was only helping. I opened the knife only to find that it wasn't a knife. It was a spoon? I tried again screwdriver, again a saw, again and again. Finally, the last item left was the knife. The only thing I needed out of this contraption that Maddy claimed was one of the world's greatest inventions. I wondered how much time I had just wasted trying to find the stupid knife. I quickly started cutting away at the restraints. I had Kelly free in no time. She rubbed her wrists which were red. They were already forming bruises. Those jerks I thought to myself. My blood boiled when I thought of all the hurt they had caused.

"We need to get to your parents. They're tied up in the back of the cave," Kelly said.

"I know by the dynamite," I said solemnly.

"Why didn't you get them first?" Kelly asked little stunned but also touched.

I wasn't sure what to say. I mean I haven't seen my parents for 12 years. I don't really know them and even though I now know the reason it was still a tough pill to swallow. I feel closer to Kelly because she had raised me, protected me, and guided me these last 12 years. I noticed that Shawna wasn't in a hurry to get to her parents either. She looked a bit anxious and even nervous. I needed to go talk to her. So I turned to Kelly. She seemed to read my face and know what I was feeling and thinking. She was always so good at reading me. She knew me better than I even knew myself at times

"Go talk to her," Kelly said before I could even try to form words.

I went over to Shawna. She had tears in her eyes.

"I don't know if I can face them. I mean they left me. I can't forgive them. I have tried Sebastian. But I just can't. Shawna spoke so quietly so deflated. I barely heard her and yet I knew the immense strength it took to whisper out those powerful feelings. I had feelings similar to hers. But I wasn't sure exactly how to put them into words. I felt selfish and was battling against those feelings. I was trying to pull back and look at the big picture but the camera kept zooming right back to the fact that they left me. Maddy walked over along with Dimitri. Tyler was busy giving Lucas small sips of water as Kelly was gingerly cleaning his bloody wounds. There was a glint in Kelly's eyes. I had not yet seen this before. Lucas seemed to notice it too. I could tell because despite being so banged up he was smiling. Not a silly smile but instead a satisfied grin. In that moment I could see that they had forgiven each other and allowed their pride to melt away. It was as if it was just the two of them in the whole wide world and nothing else mattered except for that moment.

Lucas reached into his pocket and pulled out Kelly's missing earring. Tears now freely flowed down her cheeks as well as Lucas's. I felt guilty being here in their moment but it was so incredible to be a part. A moment so long waited for. Maddy's voice snapped me out of Lucas and Kelly's world back to my own.

"Look I understand you're upset. Your parents left you I get it. But they were protecting you. They thought it was the right thing to do. In a perfect world, things could be different but as we know this is not a perfect world. The Corp. and VI-

The count is very much alive and manipulating things. At least your parents are alive," Maddy said a bit coldly.

Although I thought this to be unintentional. I could tell that she didn't mean to be so harsh by the facial expression she made afterward. I know she's full of hurt and sadness so I didn't take it personally.

"Maddy's right. Our parent's fault and look what happened to them. We were taken away and they…" Dimitri drifted off.

He didn't need to finish his train of thought. A pang of guilt reawakened in my gut. The situation was so difficult, so confusing, so overwhelming. Kelly and Lucas joined in beside us. Kelly spoke up first.

"We are all in this together," As she said this she gave a warm smile at Lucas.

This is what Lucas wanted from the beginning.

His blue eyes were full of pride and tears as he chimed in "We are stronger together!"

With that, we all walked further back into the cave. The light was low but we could still make out the four figures over in the back corner. The stack of boxes containing the dynamite was over Lucas's head. VI-Count was counting on no survivors. This cave wouldn't even hold up to the amount of power in those boxes. As we got closer we could hear the murmurs. But we were not able to make out the words due to the gags in their mouths. Shawna approached her mother and undid her gag as well as her blindfold. When she did Maya let out a gasp. She recognized Shawna instantly. Her feisty temperament shined through right away. As her cool gray eyes shot from each one of us to the other.

Then she spoke, "What are you doing here? Get out of here! They will be back any minute to blow this place up whether you're still in it or not!"

"Nice to see you too, MOM!" Shawna said with a lot of attitude, matching and returning her mother's feistiness.

"Don't give me that attitude Shawna!" Maya said coldly, her grey eyes seemed cold.

"Oh no, you lost that right to boss me around or try to parent me when you left," Shawna shouted.

Maya was taken aback and grew quiet. Her

overly confident tall slender build shrinking. Malcolm already had his gag and blindfold removed watching the horrifying scene play out before him. He seemed even shorter in the low light of the cave. His black hair grayed with the passage of time. He was no longer clean-shaven. I feel bad for Malcolm because he didn't want to join the rebellion unlike Maya, Shawan's mother.

Malcolm spoke so softly, "I'm sorry baby. We never wanted any of this to happen…"

"Well it did, and you can't change that," Shawna shouted cutting off her father.

Not backing down and refusing to be consoled. Shawna was so upset. All the emotions she had stuffed over the years came boiling over uncontrollably. Kelly took Shawna by the shoulder and led her away from her parents to let her cool down. I could hear her sobbing off in the distance trying to explain to Kelly something that she would never be able to fully understand. Malcolm and Lucas had already untied my mother and father's gags and blindfolds. I can smell a familiar scent of mechanical grease and sweat wafting through the air. I thought to myself how could that scent be so familiar even though

it was so long ago? His golden brown eyes looked
at me so tenderly it cut through me.
He seemed to be so careful not wanting
the same outcome as Maya and Malcolm had
received from Shawna. It seemed that as another
rebel leader, he did not want to make the same
mistake. He did not want to light a fuse that could
not be put out. Then I paused, I saw my mom's
ocean-like blue eyes and dark complexion
complemented by her peaceful smile. Although
there were more wrinkles than the memory of her
in my mind.

She still had her short wavy dark brown hair.
Although the dark brown hair had some gray. My
father had aged the most. His light brown hair
was completely greyed on the sides and
peppered through the top. I suppose being one
of the rebel liters wasn't a stress-free life. The
knots in my stomach are tighter. I really didn't
know what to say. I had thought for so long that
they were dead. But here they are in front of me. I
couldn't deny it. My father's light complexion
almost glowed in the low light. I had a hard time
sleeping many nights running through my mind

what I would say, how I would react, and even trying to figure out how I would feel in this moment. But I felt nothing but numb. Unable to find words. Lucas broke the silence which I was grateful for.

"Emmett, where are all the others," Lucas asked, trying to redirect the tension in the room.

"I am not sure. I heard the Watchman talking about how they were going to bring them here," Emmett said.

He now wore a focused and determined face, leaving behind the one from moments ago, the one of uncertainty.

"We didn't even know they were onto us. They caught us in the Dome when we were going to leave the final directions for the uprising, " Stella said somberly.

"Lord Byron has been watching me. I had no idea. This is all my fault. I have been putting everyone in danger and jeopardizing our mission." Lucas said frustrated with himself.

"This is not your fault! This is VI-Count and Lord Byron's fault, not yours Lucas. Do not put all this weight on your shoulders it does not belong there," Maya said firmly.

Her cool grey purpose-filled eyes seemed to be trying to drill those words into his very core.

"You have done so much for us Lucas. We could never repay you for taking care of our children all these years. Something that we should've done ourselves. If anyone is the blame it's us for putting such a huge load on your shoulders. We are so so very sorry," Malcolm said meekly.

His hazel eyes filled with tears and years of regret.

"Nonsense! You did what you had to do to protect these children. It has been a pleasure," Lucas and warmly.

Shawn and Kelly have once again joined us. I looked over at her but she wouldn't even make eye contact. I wasn't sure if she was embarrassed or if she was just still so angry.

Everyone was quiet for what seemed like forever so I spoke up, "Did everyone forget that there is a 9-foot wall of dynamite next to us?"

That seemed to snap everyone back to their senses.

"We need to plan!" Lucas said.

"Agreed!" Emmett and Maya said in unison.

I was relieved to have adults around so that they could be the ones to take over and give the instruction. It was a heavy load that I did not want at this point in my life. Maybe not ever. Seeing what it had done to my father, was heartbreaking.

Chapter 32

Emmett and Maya were off to the side talking. Lucas and Kelly came over to Shawna, Tyler, Dimitri, Maddy, and myself.

"Shouldn't Aaron, Hank, or Brutus be back by now with the rest of the Lower class members?" Tyler asked concern etched deep in his voice.

"Is this part of the trap?" asked Dimitri concerned his eyes growing wide in fear.

"It's too sloppy. VI-Count has never let his guard down. Something must have gone wrong. We have to get back to the Dome and we have to do it now!" Lucas said this with a sudden urgency in his voice.

"What's wrong Lucas? What do you know that you are not telling us?" Kelly asked as she picked up on Lucas's alarm.

"There's no time to explain right now! Follow me!" Lucas commanded.

No one questioned Lucas any further. We all simply followed. As we ran from the cave across the dry land back to the underground bunker. This was no easy task. Lucas was still not at 100 percent so Malcolm and My father had to assist him. The five miles felt longer this time without the easy adrenaline boost we had when going to the cave. But eventually, we made it. We were all relieved to see the hatch door still cracked open. But also alarmed. The Watchman never would have left the Dome open for outsiders to be able to infiltrate.

Luca's almost always calm face contorted into confusion and worry. When we reached the hallway of the South wing no one was in sight. No one was going in and out of their quarters. It was eerily quiet and dark. The corridors looked different to me now. Having experienced the outside world. Breathing in the air, polluted yet free. That feeling the one where I had been able to look around and see without walls or glass. The idea that I could run without coming to an end. It made the corridor smaller somehow. Harder to breathe even though the air inside was purified and clean. I have been feeling restricted. It

seemed to awaken me at my desire for freedom. One that I had never longed for before. For the last 12 years, I thought, I believed that I was free. I thought this place the Dome was home, even protection. Now I clearly see it as it truly is. A prison. A place where I have been held captive by lies and corruption. For lack of a better word, I had such a yucky feeling inside taking over me. To now see and know that I was manipulated all these years. I felt my breathing getting more and more shallow as the walls of the South wing closed in on me.

The gray, the lifeless gray was suffocating me. I felt myself starting to go over when Emmett my father grabbed my shoulders. His golden brown eyes were full of concern and regret. I could almost feel his remorse for all that had happened flow from his hands into me. At that moment his eyes spoke to me crying out, I'm sorry. They were pleading with me to forgive him.

But for now, it was as if he was asking a man afraid of heights to climb the Empire State Building. My knees were growing weak. I was trying to tell my lungs that they needed to take oxygen but they seemed to refuse my plea. Kelly and Shawna came by my side alarmed.

"Sebastian! I need you here with me. You are all I have. I need you. You are my best friend and I cannot do this without you. You can do this. You're stronger than you think. Do not give up. We cannot let VI-Count and Lord Byron win." Shawna pleaded with me with tears in her eyes.

I looked into her light brown eyes seeing her familiar hair doing its own thing. Even more so since Shawna had much bigger things on her mind than her hair. Then looking over at Kelly's ocean-blue eyes. Those eyes calmed my heart and my mind. My knees were no longer refusing to support me and my lungs again were doing their job.

"Thank you," I said to Shawna and Kelly.

Lucas looked over at me when I did. Once realizing I was doing better we were off again to try and find Lower class members. We were stunned when we entered the auditorium.

Chapter 33

To our surprise and amazement all the Lower-class members were already congregated in the auditorium. Somehow they had learned about VI-Counts plan! This was clear to us because everyone was gathered in the center of the auditorium confronting VI-Count and the Nobles are our supposed protectors. VI-Count himself quickly rose up from his chair on the elevated platform next to the other Nobles.

"Where is Louis? She should be up then with the other Nobles," questioned Tyler suspicion growing in his voice.

"I don't see her anywhere!" said, Lucas.

"Don't worry about Louis, she won't cause any trouble," I said a little too confidently.

This comment caused all the others to look at me with strange expressions on their faces except for Lucas. Our conversation was quickly interrupted by a furious VI-Count.

"You fools! I gave you everything you needed but you weren't satisfied. The Dome provided safety, clean air, and food. Unlike the ruined world outside. I gave you life in these protective walls!" Shouted VI-Count with anger.

I had never seen this behavior from him until now! His perfectly groomed white hair even looked a bit disheveled. His heartless grey eyes were full of rage.

"Liar!" shouted someone.

Leading to a chorus of outrage.

"You only claimed to protect us! When you were the one who took us away from our families, to begin with, and tried to make us forget them!" spat Tyler unable to control himself any longer.

"Anyone who got in your way disappeared because they would not support you and your wicked schemes. You're not a protector and this Dome doesn't offer safety. It was and is a prison. You kept us locked away from our parents from the outside. You're brainwashed us to try to make us forget. You're worse than the Corp. could ever be or ever had been!" Yelled Maddy from the top of her lungs.

Rage flared up out of her through her words and body language. The warrior was unleashed.

"You still don't see do you, imbeciles! I am the Corp!" Declared VI-Count with deep pride in his voice.

Gasps filled the auditorium at this revelation. None of us saw this coming, except maybe your parents.

"But you were supposed to protect us from the Corp!" shouted Aki who was still stunned by all that was happening to his beloved reality.

His body crumpled to the floor. Tears falling from his brown eyes. I almost felt bad for him seeing him in this state. Realization dawned on him that he was a simple tool used in VI-Counts game.

"I made a common enemy for the both of us so that we can join forces the fight against it. It was the only way to get you to join me. You hated the Corp. I hated the rebels and all those who were trying to bring my Corporation down. So I not only stopped the fighting but I also gained your trust and loyalty. With your help look at what we have become. We did this together." said VI-Count with satisfaction.

"It's all an allusion, this isn't real!" shouted a Lower class named Jonas." You are a liar!"

Just then a loud crack filled the room when a large panel broke free from the ceiling and hurled itself downward knocking VI-Count to the ground. Falling from his elevated height along with a 300-pound glass panel that crashed down with an ear-splitting shatter. Putting a sudden end to VI-Count and all his madness. Along with his plans.

Almost all in attendance stared in udder amazement as well as shock! Sheer panic filled their faces. Their bodies were tense as they grabbed their throat and chests. After a few moments when they realized that they were not going to die from the outside air that was now pouring into the Dome they relaxed their grip on their throats and chests. The chatter grew louder because unlike what they were told, they were still very much alive and able to breathe the air that we have been told was so toxic for years! A ploy that we now realize was to keep us trapped in this prison.

Everyone began to look around the room, unsure what to do now. Maybe we really do need a leader I thought to myself, everyone seems paralyzed. Lost like a sheep with a Shepard. Out of the corner of my eye, I saw Lord Byron walking in our direction. I tensed at the sight of him. He was not a small man by any means. He looked like a fright train derailed. I let out a sigh when quickly he passed us running to VI-Count. He stood there still for a moment allowing the scene to sink in. Then slowly he reached his trembling hand out and checked his leader and friend's pulse. There was no use. He wasn't going to be getting up anytime soon. Anytime ever in fact.

In a flash, Lord Byron was up in my face shouting at me. "You lousy kid! Look at what you have done."

But before he could go any further and before I could really think about it my balled-up fists made contact with his chin in a ferrous uppercut that was propelled by all the lies, frustration, and anger I had pent up inside of me from the last few weeks, no years. Resulting in Lord Byron's feet leaving the ground, soaring through the room landing directly on top of the shattered glass and VI-Count. Applause filled the room as well as the realization at the same time that it was over.

We were free. No longer under the oppressive rule of VI-Count or all his many lies. No more watchmen, no more Corp. We were safe to go and live with her parents. The outside would be able to live above ground now that the leader of the Corp. was out of commission. My mom and dad wrapped me in the tightest hug I've ever felt. To my surprise, I didn't fight it. I allowed them to hug me, and I think I might have even hugged them back.

I could hardly breathe not because of the outside air rushing in but because of the crazy happy tight hug full of relief and joy my parents were giving me. The emotion was more than I could handle. I was bawling like a baby. I stole a glance over at Shawna with her mom and dad. Tears were streaming down all of their faces as well. I felt good. We felt safe in our parent's arms for the first time in 12 years.

Our parents promised to never let us go. I didn't mind that idea I never wanted to let go either. It was an all-around happy ending if you don't consider VI-Count and the Nobles. Shawna and I had our parents. Lucas adopted Dimitri and Maddy as his own. Dimitri was thrilled to meet my father in person. He begged my father to allow him to apprentice under him as well as Lucas. My dad agreed. Tyler, well Tyler hung out with Quinn. He was the only one who seemed to be able to handle Tyler in large doses. No one could figure out how that panel mysteriously came loose from the top of the Dome.

Although, Lucas and I knew who was behind it. It was Louis one of the Nobles. She began to see how corrupt and greedy VI-Count and Lord Byron were. She did not know that he was the Corp. at the time. But she did learn how VI-Count planned to eradicate the Lower class because they were becoming a menace as Lord Byron put it to her. She also learned of the plans to use the kids to continue to work to death even if needed to finish VI-Count's plans.

She did not know everything. But she knew enough. I saw her earlier in the day on the roof. A little while later she came to me and asked to borrow a 3-inch ratchet. The exact size for the bolts that hold the glass panels in place. I didn't say a word other than you might need this too. Handing her a breaker bar because I knew those bolts could get really stuck.

Lucas and I shared a knowing look between us. But I am grateful. No one else had access to the roof panels other than VI-Count himself and the Nobles. Reflecting in my mind on what to do next I thought first I'd get out of our prison far far away from the shattered illusion and make a real life for myself.

One without brainwashing pills or an evil cruel dictator. A real-life with family. Repairing the damage from VI-Count will take time. But we have each other. Working together we can fix the damage and enjoy freedom in living life outside the Dome. After my parents let me come up for air from the longest hug recorded in human history, I put my hands in my pockets and relaxed my arms allowing a nice deep breath of air to fill my lungs. Feeling content and relieved this nightmare was finally over. I felt something in my left pocket. A piece of paper. The piece of paper that floated down on my desk from the vent. I had totally forgotten about it. I was going to read it with Shawna. I almost crumbled it and threw it away. Since all of this was over, the truth was out. But curiosity got the best of me.
It read…

I NEED YOUR HELP! I KNOW THEY ARE WATCHING LUCAS! I CAN NOT DO THIS ALONE. RELEASE QUINN FROM THE UNDERGROUND DUNGEON. I HAVE GIVEN HIM INSTRUCTIONS TO WHERE THE 92 CARP MEMBERS ARE. THEY HAVE MADDY, TYLER, DIMITRI'S PARENTS IMPRISONED. ALONG WITH THE OTHER OUTSIDERS AS WELL AS QUINN'S FATHER TOBEY. WE NEED TO STOP THEM. THEY PLAN ON DESTROYING THE DOME. ACT QUICKLY BEFORE IT IS TO LATE? WE WILL NEED YOUR SKILL SEBASTIAN IF WE ARE GOING TO BE SUCCESSFUL.
-LOUIS

That free feeling of contentment and calm was replaced with dread and panic. As I walked over to Lucas to hand him the letter from Louis. Realizing we were not yet free.